Second Touch

Adrian Harding

HOPE SERIES, Volume One. July 2016.

Caribbean Chapters Publishing Inc.
P.O. Box 8050, Oistins, Christ Church, Barbados
www.caribbeanchapters.co

ISBN (paperback): 978-976-8265-61-6

Thank you Jesus for the
strength and grace to share
your message of Hope.

I pray that you would minister
to all who read this book.

Preface

Have you ever wondered why life is the way it is, with all its ups and downs, highs and lows, ins and outs? Many people say 'life is not fair' and to some degree there is a measure of truth to this statement. But what is fairness? Is it not strange that life can hand one person a bag of promises so that he/she excels and blooms like the flowers, and yet hand the same bag of promises to another person who wastes it?

In my interaction with people, I have realized that some adults are not sure of what they are passionate about and some 'feel' something, but are not sure what it is. It is my hope that when you read this book you will be inspired to find your passion and pursue it.

This story is about a boy named Kevin, who from a young age discovered his passion, joy and love for playing cricket. He decided that this was what he wanted to do for the rest of his life, and nothing or no one would prevent him from accomplishing this goal.

The story commences with a look at Kevin's early life, but also gives insight into early Barbadian life—the days when there was no indoor water or electricity, and eating food cooked on the stove in the yard was a normal activity. It reflects on Kevin's growth in a village where family life was very closely knit and everybody knew everybody.

Although this book is meant to encourage us to follow our dreams, we should never forget the important aspects of our lives—God, family life and one's own sense of being.

My hope is that as you read this book you will come to the acknowledgement that all is not lost… look up, smell the air, hear the birds… THERE IS HOPE! So come and meet Kevin on his walk through this journey we call life, and always remember: As long as there is life, there is Hope!

It is never too late to start over.

Thanks to my wife Shelly-Ann, and my entire
family who generously supported me in
writing this book.
Thank you for your time and patience.

Special thanks to Tedroy Daniel, Sandra
Squires and Jackie Norville for their insights
and to the others who have helped.

Most of all, thanks to God for his creativity,
revelation, ability and strength to work
tirelessly to create this book so that
his message of love can be generated
through a story.

Table of Contents:

This is a work of fiction.

Names, characters, businesses,
places, events and incidents are either
products of the author's imagination or
used fictitiously.

Any resemblance to actual persons,
living or dead, or actual events or
locales, is purely coincidental.

1...Early Life

Kevin woke up on Saturday morning, earlier than usual, to go and look for his ball which got lost the day before while he and his friends Barry, Bruce and Jasper were playing cricket with Timmy and his friends, who were from the neighboring village, on the big pasture late into the evening. Kevin realized that outside was still relatively dark and he could hardly see a thing. As he stumbled around the house looking for his old shoes, trying to be as quiet as possible, he became angry as he reflected on how Timmy had lost his ball and if he did not find it Kevin wouldn't be able to play cricket; and nothing made Kevin angrier than not being able to play cricket. He lived and breathed cricket and he would play it all day long if he could.

Timmy was batting when Bruce bowled a ball

which he could not resist hitting hard. Timmy hit it so hard that it went sky high and when it landed and bounced no one saw where it went.

"We told you don't hit the ball so hard when outside is dark!" shouted Jasper, who was the smallest boy in the group but had the loudest voice. "And now we can't play anymore cricket!"

Timmy had made Kevin so angry that he said a few bad words. Kevin didn't usually swear, but when Timmy lost his ball it was all he could do without hitting Timmy who was bigger than him.

"You like you vex though?" said Timmy, who held up his bat and shook it at Kevin. "It was too sweet a ball not to hit hard, and if you come round me, I will lash you with this bat."

Although Timmy knew the rules which Barry who was Kevin's best friend laid down, still he insisted on always hitting the ball hard because he was strong and not afraid of the other boys.

Kevin remembered that they had searched and searched for the rest of the evening into the night, but they still could not find the ball. As he stood there still reflecting on last evening's cricket game, he couldn't believe that he was still so angry with Timmy for losing his ball. And now that he had the time to look for his ball, it was still dark outside.

"Oh man," he said, unaware of how loud he was; he had woken his mother.

"What the hell you doing up so early boy?" His mother shouted at him as she rose from her sack bed on the old wooden pine floor.

Kevin did not answer. He just stood there with his mouth shut. He knew that this was one of those questions which did not require a response.

"Answer me boy, or I will slap you."

Mother continued to shout as she searched around for something to throw at Kevin, but she could not put her hand on anything because it was still dark inside the house and she was not wearing her glasses. It did not take much to make her angry. It seemed that she went to sleep angry and woke up angry. Every day she was mad about something, and most times Kevin was at the end of the anger for her to release her frustration on.

"Sorry Ma." Kevin responded quickly.

"You should be," she retorted.

Although Kevin was still angry with Timmy

he did not dare show Mother any of it, because it only took a split second for her to throw the nearest thing that came to her hand, and Mother never missed a target.

Kevin remembered the time when she threw a large piece of ice at his cousin Marva and cut her eyebrow. And it was only because Marva called her brother an 'arse' because he would not stop teasing her about her bed-wetting.

"But auntie he was teasing me," Marva pleaded.

Although Mother was wrong for not listening, she was one of those people who never apologized, because she believed that she was always right. Kevin was convinced that she was the devil sometimes. Mother was never reluctant to share out lashes, and if she couldn't find a belt anything else would work. She would often say: "Do what I say or I will tear the blasted bark off of you."

With Mother's continual shouting and cussing, she woke everyone else in the house.

"Well, seeing that everybody up now, make no sense going back to sleep," she announced as she headed towards the kitchen to get breakfast which consisted of bakes and lemongrass tea which she had done on the yard stove the day before.

"You! Go and help your grandfather take care of those animals," Mother ordered while pointing at Kevin.

Kevin walked off, disappointed because his chance of searching for his ball was now over even before it began. His morning's routine would begin much earlier than he had anticipated.

"Well, seeing that everybody up now…" he muttered to himself, repeating Mother's words and being very careful not to let her hear him as he set off to do his usual chores.

"Me and my big mouth," he grumbled.

As Kevin exited the old white half-painted back door he looked behind him to make sure his mother did not hear him. In his haste he almost fell down the wooden steps constructed by his grandfather, but was able to balance himself quickly.

"These stupid steps," he muttered.

Sheba, Kevin's dog, ran up to him wagging her tail for her usual morning pat on the head while Brown Boy, his other dog, stayed in the comfort of the sheds because outside was still cold and he hated the cold, except for when there was food to be eaten.

Like most of the houses in Kevin's immediate neighborhood, his house was a one-roof structure with one bedroom, a kitchen, a living room and a front house that no one dared go in. That's where Mother had her "important glassware," which if anyone broke, it would spell immediate wrath for that person.

Inside the house looked dark and scary from the outside. Kevin had never noticed this before. In fact, this was the first time he was actually looking back at the house because every morning he would just do his chores and by the time he was finished the house looked normal and bright from the outside.

During the night the kerosene lamp which was left burning at a low setting was no longer shining forth its light, and re-lighting it was always mother's job. It had gone out while she was sleeping like so many times before, but once she was sleeping, no one dared to wake her. Kevin wished that they had electricity like his friend Matthias who lived way up the road. As Kevin stared into the darkened house he remembered the day he met Matthias at the beach.

"Look at that boy over there." Barry's big brother Bruce held Kevin's head and turned it towards a group of people getting out of a white car.

"Cheeze, you see his surfboard? I wish I had one," said Kevin.

"Leh we go and talk to he, maybe we could get a chance," Bruce said, and without waiting for a response from Kevin, headed over to Matthias, saying:

"I is Bruce and this is Kevin," but when he turned around Kevin was still standing over by the almond tree.

"Come and talk to Matthias!" Bruce shouted at Kevin who reluctantly came over.

"Hurry up and help wid these animals you think morning waiting on you?" Kevin was jolted back to reality as he heard his grandfather's booming voice.

Kevin continued towards the pens where his grandfather kept the animals. It was extremely cold that morning. The sun was fighting to shine through the last remaining darkness of the night, but that was no excuse for Kevin to run from his responsibilities. He was already dressed in his home clothes, which were different from the clothes he slept in because his night clothes consisted of an old pants he got from his grandfather which was so big that it fitted him like a farmer's outfit. He had planned from the night before that not even clothes would stop him from looking for his ball first thing in the morning.

He had it all figured out. *I will find my ball and then do my chores.* But that plan was quickly rearranged by his angry Mother.

The first thing he had to do even before dealing with the animals was to go to the local standpipe, which was some distance away, to bring water and fill a big barrel in the yard. The barrel was secured to a big old golden apple tree which his Uncle Frank had planted next to the pit toilet.

The water in the barrel was used for anything outside the house and for bathing. Kevin's grandfather, Pops, who thought of himself as a 'jack of all trades', had connected a piece of pipe to the barrel which led into the yard bathroom and acted as a shower.

It usually took Kevin five to six trips to fill the

big barrel, but because of his urgent need to find his green ball, he filled the barrel in four trips. It was a hard task because it required that he carry bigger buckets, but he was determined, for he had an objective in mind, which was to play cricket that evening by any means necessary.

"I don't know why Pops got so many animals." He muttered as he hurried to feed his grandfather's animals which consisted of six pigs, ten rabbits, forty chickens and some yard fowls. Then he took the eight sheep out to the big pasture to a selected area which was far away from the cricket pitch.

Pops' responsibility was to take the cows down to the gully where they could graze and find shelter in the shade of the trees, because they were too big for Kevin to handle, especially Betsy. But all the while Kevin thought about his ball, and if he didn't find it there would be no cricket that evening, and that was all Kevin wanted to do—play cricket.

He had dreams of one day making it big and had already established firmly in his mind that nothing or no one would stand in his way of reaching the top. His role model began as a poor boy and was now a very great cricketer. Kevin imagined that one day he would be like that also; playing cricket all over the world. Even if the other boys didn't want to play cricket, he and Barry played by themselves, sometimes on the big pasture or between the houses.

"If wunna lick out any uh my windows I gine brek up that bat!" Mother would often threatened.

"Just hit de ball low," Barry advised.

All of this was just preparation for him because he believed that one day he would be a great cricketer.

2...Big Bad Billy

It was Saturday. This meant that there was no school and that made Kevin extremely glad. He would not have to run from Big Bad Billy who was always teasing him and threatening to push him down the hill into the nearby swamp.

Billy was big, really big, and for a boy of only ten years of age he was the biggest child in the whole school and Kevin felt he was also the meanest.

Billy lived up on the hill with his father Joe, just around the corner from the school that Kevin attended. During lunch time Big Bad Billy would beat up the other children and take away their money and lunch and threaten to beat them some more if they told on him. He was especially angry because Kevin could play cricket and he could not. He had tried many times before, but failed miserably.

However, if any of the boys wanted to learn anything about the types of fish in the swamp, Billy was the person to go to. If they wanted to learn how to fish he was the expert, spending many days at the swamp fishing and looking for crabs with Lil' Man Sam. Lil' Man Sam was Billy's right hand man, and followed Billy everywhere.

"How come you could fish so good?" Sam asked Billy one morning during school vacation.

Without blinking Billy gave him a hard slap behind his head and shouted: "I thought I told you to stop asking me the same question more than two times!"

Billy was very upset and was supposed to correct Sam by saying "more than one time," but he was not even aware he had made a mistake. One-foot Mike, who was on the other side of the swamp relaxing, heard everything. He got on his bike and immediately went and told Suzie.

Mike was an interesting character, and the people in the village could not figure out how he was able to ride a bicycle with one foot, but he had developed a technique which was fascinating to observe. He would sit on the saddle, place his crotch on the handle and the bar, push off with his foot, and wait until the pedals came around and push again; this was his way of getting around the village.

When Suzie, who was the village's chief gossiper, heard what Billy said and did to Sam, she quickly circulated the news around the village and school. Suzie always had a way of changing up a story so that the way she told it was very different from the way she heard it from Mike. Her version was:

"You hear that Lil' Man slapped Billy because he won't stop asking the same question?"

As Kevin continued his chores, he paused for a moment from staking out the sheep as he reflected on the time Big Bad Billy pulled his ears so hard that he heard bells for the rest of the day. Kevin did not tell his grandfather about that time, because his grandfather was a 'piece of a madman', as all the members of Kevin's family would often say, and it only took one word about anybody talking bad to or hurting Kevin for Pops' to go for his cutlass. Kevin was Pops' favorite, and he had no problem letting the other siblings know.

I wish Billy would get sting by Pa-Pa Brown's honey bees, thought Kevin. Papa Brown lived way up the hill on the other side of the big pasture and was famous for his bee-keeping skills and sweet honey.

Kevin was suddenly brought back to reality as he heard his grandfather's voice: "Boy you dreaming again?"

"No Pops," answered Kevin as he rushed to finish staking out the last two sheep.

He then headed back through the gate with every intention of bathing his two dogs and himself, only to realize that everyone in the house had used all the water he'd brought not long ago. This made Kevin angry for the second time that morning.

"Who use up all the water?" he shouted, but no one answered.

This meant he would have to go to the standpipe again and bring water. He however decided against it and instead planned to take his bath at the local standpipe.

"Those dogs can get bathe later," he said to himself.

The sun was really shining when Kevin finished

doing his chores, and finally he had the rest of the day to search for his green ball. Kevin quietly eased away from home just hoping that Mother would not call upon him to do something else. It seemed like he was the only one to ever get called upon to do chores. Although Uncle Frank had two children they seemed to be exempt from chores. Even his Uncle never did anything in or around the house. All Kevin knew was that his uncle planted the golden apple tree.

Since he was laid off from the sugar plantation, Uncle Frank never worked another day in his life and spent every waking moment at the rum shop hoping to drink rum with the boys. His wife Gloria became so frustrated that she left him and the children one rainy day and never returned. Frank was devastated. He was mother's older brother and he was just a big waste, and Pops would often cuss him out. But Frank never answered back, he would just walk off smiling.

As Kevin was easing past the sheep pen he heard Pops talking to Uncle Frank:

"You are the laziest man I know. I should have gone to the bathro…" Pops was about to finish saying something really nasty to Frank when he remembered that Kevin was around; but little did he know that Kevin was on his search for his ball.

Kevin looked everywhere he thought the ball could go. He even climbed the nearby clamacherry trees on the outskirts of the pasture to see if by chance it was stuck in the branches. That was his only ball. In fact it was his favorite ball, and he had bowled out all the boys in the neighborhood with it. Kevin loved that ball so much that he named it 'Girlie'. Girlie was lost on two occasions before, but they found it in time to still play cricket. Timmy was really strong and had hit it really hard. Kevin hoped that one day he could hit the ball as hard as Timmy.

He even went as far as the shop to look for it, but after forty five minutes of searching for his ball, it still remained lost.

"Where this stupid ball is?" He spoke out of frustration.

The only place left to look was over by Ms. Prescott, but that was a no-no, because her dog was cruel and vicious and even if his ball was near her paling, he was not going there. However, his love for his ball and his desperate need to play cricket drove him to do the unthinkable. So like a cat ready to corner a mouse, he silently eased his way close to her paling and peeped through a hole. Unbelievably, he saw it. At last Kevin had found his ball after hours of searching; it had somehow found its way into Ms. Prescott's yard and was right in the middle of her flower bed. Kevin ran back over to his house and blurted out.

"Cheese don bread, why of all de places this ball gone over by she house? All de time I looking, and look where it is."

Ms. Prescott was not at home. She had left early that morning to go to the market to buy meat for herself and the dog, which was part of her family. She had no children and her dog was like a son to her. It was even allowed to go into the house. Kevin eased over again by her paling and peeped through the hole one more time, and this time he saw the dog sniffing the air as if it smelt something. Then suddenly the dog rushed to the hole where Kevin was and started barking at the paling.

Kevin jumped back and ran home.

3...The Rescue

It was clear that retrieving his ball would be no walk in the park. Lion the bull-mastiff dog would make sure of it. Kevin had to devise a plan to get his ball without Lion getting him. Time was getting on and he wanted to play cricket, so he came up with a clever plan he called the 'Fly Trap'. It was a modified version of the one he and his best friend Barry used to catch birds and Ms. Bay-Bay's chickens and guinea fowls, but this was designed to catch Ms. Prescott's Bull-Mastiff dog Lion. This was no ordinary bird- or chicken-catching event because unlike birds and chickens, dogs can bite.

Kevin started working immediately on constructing the lasso, but he needed some bait to lure Lion into the trap. So he stole a piece of his mother's chicken from the pot while she was busy gossiping over by Mr. Harris the next door neighbor, and was glad that he wasn't caught, because surely she would have beaten him severely.

As he was hurrying back to his creation he lifted his shirt to help ease the burning pain in his hand caused by the hot chicken, and to also catch the dripping sauce which was leaving a trail of evidence on the ground. Quickly he found an old pot and lifted it onto the work bench and dropped the chicken in it, while warning his dogs: "Touch it and die."

He changed his shirt and had hurried back to clean up any signs that he was by Mother's pot, but he was elated to discover that Brown Boy, one of his dogs, had done the 'clean up' job for him.

"You know this half o' idiot brother of mine left hey every since morning to go by de shop to drink rum?" Mother was still talking with Mr. Harris, but she was no longer over by his house and she was much nearer to the stove when Kevin quietly returned to clean any evidence by the stove area.

"Lil boy wha de ass you doing by my stove?"
Mother startled Kevin as she turned around
quickly.

"I was just trying to help with the wood 'cause
it was gine out." Kevin used his imagination
quickly to avoid a lash from her.

"Get from there you fool… before I throw you
in the pot!" Mother shouted.

Kevin obeyed and rushed off, returning to
complete his invention. When he was finished
he threw all the remaining evidence which
would link him to chicken into an old bag and
hid it among the garbage at the back of the shed,
then quickly ran over by Ms. Prescott's paling
and threw the lasso into the yard. When Lion
rushed for the chicken, Kevin caught him with
one attempt. Lion was so engrossed with the
chicken that he didn't even realize that a rope
was around his neck.

The hardest part was securing the other end
of the rope to the nearest tree, which happened
to be a lime tree, just in case Lion finished the
chicken before he got his ball.

"Ow, ow these things real pointy," he said
softly as he tied the knot around the lime tree.

Kevin was not taking any chances with Lion. While Lion was busy with the bone Kevin jumped down into the yard, retrieved his ball, climbed back over the paling and ran as fast as he could, leaving Lion behind to find his way out of his trap. He was still breathing hard when he almost knocked down Pops coming through the gate.

"You running from a steel donkey?" Pops asked.

"No Sir. I was just testing my speed," Kevin replied and ran off to avoid any more questions.

"Wait you ain't want this?" Pops asked while bending to pick up the ball. Kevin was already turning because he realized that he had dropped Girlie, his favorite ball, which he had risked his life only moments ago to retrieve.

4...Billy Gets It

After retrieving his ball from behind Ms. Prescott's paling and his encounter with Pops it was after 1 o' clock in the afternoon. Kevin went over to Barry's house, which was about five houses away from his, to share the great news.

"Barry I find Girlie!"

"Where you find it?" Barry asked Kevin.

"I can't tell you, I frighten that even the birds gine hear."

"But we is best friends."

"I know, I will tell you later."

"So what we gine do till cricket time?"

"Leh we pitch marbles."

So they cleared an area of dirt away from under the cherry tree and started to play 'knuckles'. This was a pitching game in which any of the boys became the loser if he was unable to get his marble into the hole on the ground, and he would receive hits on his knuckles from a marble by the winner or winners. Barry was very good at the game and was winning, but lost concentration when Kevin asked:

"Barry you feel we still gine be friends when we grow up?"

"It depends on if we like de same girl." Barry said jokingly.

"But you don't even like girls," Kevin responded and then shouted: "I win!"

"You distracted me!" Barry responded in disbelief.

Evening took forever to come, but when it finally came there was nothing that could stop Kevin from playing cricket now that he had found Girlie.

As usual, Kevin was batting first and once he had the bat there was not much chance of anybody else getting a batting hand. That evening Billy was on the field as a catcher only because he and Timmy had a bet who could catch the best, otherwise he would be home fixing his fishing rods. Bruce was just about to bowl another spin ball. Suddenly he stopped, and cricket came to a halt around 6:30 pm when Ms. Prescott came barging through her yard gate onto the pasture with a big bamboo stick in her hand, shouting:

"Who is the so-and-so that tie up my dog Lion? And who mash up my flower bed jumping over my paling?"

All the boys looked at each other in total shock, but could not answer Ms. Prescott. They could not imagine who would be crazy enough to take a chance with Lion, or even with Ms. Prescott.

Ms. Prescott was walking past Billy, still angry. Immediately Kevin knew that this was the perfect opportunity to get back at Big Bad Billy for pulling his ears.

"It was Big Bad Billy!" Kevin shouted out and pointed at Billy. "It was he and Sam, but Billy, he jumped over the paling."

Before Billy could say a word to defend himself, Ms. Prescott turned around and put two hot lashes in his backside with the bamboo stick.

"But it…" before Billy could say another word, two more were in his shoulder blades. Ms. Prescott was fast with the stick and made another swing at Billy, who was already on the run.

All the boys started to laugh when Billy took off running for home like a speeding bullet with Sam trying to catch up. They had never seen Big Bad Billy run so fast until his pants dropped down. Ms. Prescott was still furious and took off running after him, but Billy was way too quick for her, so she returned to the rest of the boys panting like a dog and said with a threatening voice:

"Don't come over at my place." Then she marched off cussing and swearing.

Outside was getting dark and Kevin could hear in the distance his grandfather's yard fowls announcing that night time was near as they flew up into the big tamarind tree at the back of the house. The boys headed for their houses, still laughing.

Although Billy was bad to him in the past, Kevin felt sorry for him and wished that he had not told that lie, but he knew that if he had admitted it was him, then he would surely be a cripple by morning time. He was not a big boy like Billy. He would never have survived those lashes.

Bright and early the following morning, a

Sunday, Ms. Prescott had Lion outside the paling tied on a long chain, preventing passersby from venturing near her paling. When Lion saw Kevin he almost popped the chain trying to get him, because he remembered the distinct smell of blue soap which Kevin bathed with. But Kevin was fast and ran around the back of Mr. Herbert's house just in time, preventing Ms. Prescott from recognizing who it was that caused her dog to behave that way.

That was close, Lion almost had me. If I didn't get up early to go and look for some sticks for mother to cook with I would never find out that Ms. Prescott gone mad tying her dog like that. Kevin thought to himself.

That only heightened his already alerted senses, because he was on the lookout for Big Bad Billy. At any sign of him Kevin was ready to run, but that entire day Billy was nowhere to be seen. In fact, for two days no one saw or heard Big Bad Billy and no one even dared to go over by his place. Rumours began to circulate that Billy was going to get Kevin if it was the last thing he did. This made Kevin the most uneasy person on planet earth, because he could not begin to imagine what a big boy like Billy would do to a small boy like him… until one Sunday morning when Kevin felt this big hand around his neck as he was lifted high in the air and pushed down the hill into the swamp.

"That is for lying and tomorrow will be for the pain in my back!" Billy shouted.

Kevin felt every roll down the hill. He could not even prevent it from happening. Then like a big rock he landed in the water. Good thing he landed near the edge, because legend had it that there was quick sand in the middle of the swamp and one or two persons disappeared after falling into the center of the swamp. Kevin tried to move his leg, but it was stuck in the mud. After a few minutes of pulling it became free, but as he stood up it felt like every place in his body hurt. Slowly he tried to get out of the swampy water but fell again as a sharp pain shot through his right leg.

I hope my foot ain't brek, he thought.

The pain in his leg was radiating up to his back, so he reached behind to rub his back and heard a snap, and was elated to know that it was not coming from his aching body, but from a broken branch which fell at the same time.

Pops gine get Billy when I tell him what just happen, Kevin thought to himself.

The hot Sunday sun was drying the mud on his body fast and he needed to get to the standpipe, but that would require climbing the hill and with his leg still paining it seemed an impossible task. As he sat in the water contemplating his next move the small fish swam up to his hands and nibbled at his mossy fingers.

"I need to get out of this water," he spoke out loud and then dragged himself out of the muddy water.

5...The Encounter

Finally Kevin was out of the swampy water. He was covered in mud and moss from head to toe. Feeling exhausted, he sat on the ground and waited until he regained some measure of strength and to make sure Billy was not there, then he painfully tried to stand and wobbled a bit, but was soon able to put some pressure on his right foot as he stood upright. The hill before him looked like a mountain. Slowly he approached it, climbed and limped towards the standpipe.

Kevin was not even aware that there were a number of girls who saw what happened and were watching as he painfully walked to the standpipe. One girl startled him as she shouted:

"If that was me, I would have kicked him where the sun doesn't shine!"

Kevin turned around quickly and was totally embarrassed, not because of what the girl said, but standing with the girls was Jan Matthews, on her way home from church. She was the most beautiful girl that Kevin had ever seen. She had the smoothest black skin and her hair was always long and in two sections and she always wore blue ribbons at the end of her hair. Her clothes were never wrinkled and her shoes were always clean, and because it was Sunday she looked extremely beautiful.

Ignoring the pain in his body, Kevin lifted his chest as if to suggest he was okay, for this was the girl of his dreams. He had wished on many occasions that he could to talk to her, but he was never brave enough. Now he was sure that she would have nothing to do with him, so he held his head down again and shamefully continued to limp towards the pipe, but to his surprise she said:

"It's okay Kevin, we won't tell anyone, right girls?"

"Whatever you say Jan," they said and walked off, leaving Kevin and Jan alone.

Kevin had dreamt about this moment for so

many nights and days. In his dreams he was dressed in nice clothes and clean shoes, not in moss and mud. Kevin opened his mouth to say something that he thought would somehow change the situation and convince Jan that he slipped and fell into the swamp when he was about to jump-kick Billy, but all that came out was:

"You know my name?"

"Yes," she said, "and I have been watching you for a long time playing cricket and I think that you have a great future ahead."

Kevin could not answer. For the first time in his entire life he actually had no words. Jan followed him as he continued walking to the pipe. She stayed a distance off and thought about what she could say to him next. She had wanted to talk to Kevin for a long time also, but the opportunity was never allowed her until now. Therefore, ignoring her fear of rejection, she allowed the natural feeling of attraction to take its course.

Meanwhile, washing the mud off, Kevin pinched himself to see if he was dreaming. Although he was in pain this still had to be a dream because here was the perfect girl talking to him; the girl he had envisioned sweeping off her feet with his smile and charm, but now that she was right next to him he could not say a word.

"Can you teach me how to play cricket?" Jan asked deliberately, trying to take Kevin's mind off his embarrassment.

"If you want," he replied confidently as the shame and embarrassment began to wear off.

Jan waited until Kevin was clean and then they left the standpipe, talking some more as he headed home and she to her parents' house.

Big Bad Billy never had the courage to put his threat into action after Kevin's grandfather found out what he did to Kevin.

Kevin walked through the always-open gate as if he was on cloud nine because he just had the best moment of his life talking with Jan Matthews. The pain and embarrassment of what Big Bad Billy did to him was mild compare to the joy he was feeling. Kevin was so happy that Mother startled him when she said:

"You clothes very wet lil' boy," as she stood scratching her head because she could not remember when it was raining.

"Big Bad Billy pushed me in the swamp," Kevin replied.

Pops immediately appeared as if from nowhere and announced: "I gine over by he house now and deal wid he."

But before Pops left he went to the shed and got his cutlass and started to sharpen the already sharp blade, all the while talking to himself.

"He touch Kevin… Well I gine burst in he tail or my name ain't Theodore Bratts."

Kevin followed behind as his grandfather headed over to Billy's house. Billy was outside fixing his fishing pole.

"You stay hey," he said to Kevin and approached Billy.

Unknown to Pops, Billy's father was sitting in the doorway of the old house and got up when he heard Pop's voice. He quickly went inside and closed the door, because he had had an encounter with Pops fifteen years earlier and it ended with him tasting the edge of Pops' cutlass on the back of his foot. No one could understand how Pops cut Billy's father's foot, but some said he was really afraid of Pops.

Pops didn't use his sword that day. Instead he had a few words with Billy right in his ear. Kevin saw Pops' lips moving fast, so he knew a few explicit adjectives or verbs were escaping. No one knew what conversation transpired between them, so for the rest of the school term Kevin and Billy stayed far away from each other.

"Only me can tear the skin off of you; anybody else touch you I will chop them to pieces." Pops said to Kevin later that evening.

"Pops, Billy father real frighten fa you. Wha you do him?" Kevin asked.

"He stole a sheep from me and told me I can't do nothing about it," Pops replied.

"So that's why you chop he foot?"

"I did want to tek it off, but I change my mind and just leh he feel a lil' o' de power."

As Pops and Kevin laughed about the whole situation, they headed to the pasture to bring in the animals.

The next day there was a lot of talk in the village and at school that Pops cut Billy really badly and he almost died, but that was only a rumor that Suzie generated. A few loved it, but most of the villagers knew otherwise. Billy was so shaken by the whole incident that he even stopped bullying the other children and he was the first out of the school gate that evening and every evening when school was finished.

6...Real focus

After their initial meeting and conversation, Kevin and Jan spent a lot of time together and news began to spread like cane fire that Kevin and Jan were 'boyfriend and girlfriend'.

Besides cricket, Jan was the next best thing that ever happened to him. She was not only a source of laughter, but of great encouragement. Kevin was not happy at home with his mother and would often talk to Jan about the unfairness in his house.

"You believe that this morning my mother gave my food to the dogs, because I stayed too long in the bath?" Kevin confided in Jan.

"Don't worry, one of these days it won't happen no more," she said to him.

Even though Jan was just fourteen years old

(and Kevin twelve), she showed a remarkable strength that way surpassed her peers. In fact, she was so extraordinary that Kevin could not believe that she was his girl, but she saw something in Kevin that caused her to grow more fond of him and even though they were still young, they both knew that they wanted to be together.

Because of their friendship, many of Jan's girlfriends stopped speaking to her because they could not understand how she could have a boyfriend like Kevin.

"How you could like he? He ain't got nothing. I want a man that got nuff money," Veronica said to her one day at school.

"I know you think so, but what I see you don't. And besides I like him a lot."

Although Kevin was not raised by his father, he had certain principles that he followed even at such a young age. He was focused and not sidetracked by the boys who were just interested in parties and smoking. Kevin wanted to do his school work well and play cricket. Besides, mother and pops had already told him that if he used cigarettes or any other drug that together they would beat him with a piece of bamboo branch.

Unlike Kevin, Jan was being raised by a mother and father and she was not like the other girls, looking for love in all the wrong places. Jan's father was a respectable man in the village and many looked to him for guidance. He was not a doctor or lawyer, but he was an elder in the church and was always talking about the Bible. Jan was a member of that church and she sang in the choir. Whenever there was a special occasion, which was often, the pastor would ask Jan to sing a solo which always caused such an emotional stir throughout the congregation. Although Kevin was not a church boy he would often stop by the church and listen to Jan singing, making sure of course that she never saw him.

"Barry she sound real sweet," Kevin would say.

"Yes Kevin, but you better be careful 'round she cause I hear that she fadda got a gun and shoot a boy already in he foot fa peeping through the paling at she when she was bathing,"

Barry warned Kevin one Sunday.

"So how come I never hear so?"

"I ain't got your ears."

At school Jan was the envy of a lot of girls because Jan's parents, although they were not rich, took a special interest in her appearance. She was never heard shouting or quarrelling and was very selective in choosing her friends.

Kevin knew what sort of man Jan's father was, and therefore he made sure that he always 'dotted his I's and crossed his T's'. After playing cricket one evening, Jan's father approached Kevin on the big pasture and said to him:

"Watch yourself, 'cause if you hurt my baby I coming for you."

Jan was special to Kevin, and he did not need to be threatened, although even after a whole school's term of being friends he did not yet comprehend how she could like him and sometimes he would ask her:

"Why of all the boys you like me?"

She would reply: "I don't know how to explain it, you are just different."

Jan tried on many occasions to explain her devotion for Kevin to her friends, but they could not understand. However, this never weakened her resolve because she loved Kevin and he loved her. None of the other girls or boys tried to come between them because they saw that the bond was inseparable. Jan and Kevin were like two peas in a pod and were seldom seen apart when at school.

Jan even taught Kevin how to play music on the recorder and they spent time practicing together. Soon after they formed a school band called the 'J and K Band', which did well for a while, but then it was not Kevin's first love and after a while the band dissolved as Kevin became more and more dedicated to cricket.

After school in the evening the cricket coach made sure that Kevin was learning all he could about the game.

"It is not just about playing cricket; it is about knowing cricket," said the coach to the boys.

Many times Mother would come to the school quarrelling with Kevin.

"You live out here? It is time to come home."

Kevin would obey, but he would somehow forget the next time and stay out late playing cricket because time was not important; darkness was not an issue; not even rain was a reason to stop playing cricket. Once Kevin could still see the ball, the game had to go on. All the boys on the team were like this, but they didn't take it as seriously as Kevin did. It seemed as if he was built for cricket. He learnt it so quickly.

What was giving the other boys a challenge was a no-brainer for Kevin. There was a confidence he had that many misinterpreted as pride or arrogance, but Kevin did not care what people thought or said about him. He had a dream to be the best cricketer.

"Martin Luther had a dream and he believed in it; don't let nobody take yours."

Pops was famous for telling Kevin this. Kevin never forgot those words. They seemed to be printed onto his brain and he would often recite them to whoever was challenging him to stop playing so much cricket.

One day at school a boy became angry at Kevin because he could not get Kevin bowled out and said: "You always feel that you should bat de longest!"

"Martin Luther had a dream and he believed in it; I won't let you or nobody take mine. So because you can't bat you trying to stop me." Kevin replied and continued batting.

Kevin was not short on words when it came to defending the game and his love for it. He was often heard arguing with others about who was the greatest at playing cricket and who was not. Not only was he passionate about cricket, but if he felt he was right about anything else he would state his view on what he thought it should or should not be.

"De old people was right. Ya can't put words in you mout'." Fisherman Dan said to him one day when Kevin argued that cricket was the best sport ever.

Kevin was a thinker and confident; some said he was just like his mother while others said like his grandfather. However, most agreed that he was just like Pops his grandfather who was also a sports expert and Kevin's source of encouragement. Pops would often sit and talk with Kevin about life and Kevin especially liked when he shared about the good old days. Pops was more of a father than grandfather to Kevin, and therefore Kevin did not feel bad that he never knew his real father. According to his mother, Kevin's father was an ass. She hated him and would often speak to Kevin as if it was his fault that his father was not around. One day, during one of Pops' talks with him, he asked:

"Who is my father?"

"Don't tell you mother I tell you this, but you look just like him." Pops said.

"What is his name?" Kevin asked.

"Boy, you putting me in some deep trouble." Pops said.

"But he got to have a name."

"He name is Kevin."

"I got he name?" Kevin asked in disbelief.

"Yes, but if you tell your mother I say so I will bury you in the back by the cows." Pops threatened.

Kevin was not going to tell, but he could not help but wonder why a man would give his son his name and not be around to see him grow. Kevin wanted his father around, but he never really missed him. As they say: "You don't miss what you never had."

Kevin did not dwell much on it, because cricket was always on his mind along with Jan Matthews, so as far as he was concerned what people said about him was not important; not even so much what his mother said was important. Pops was proud of him and that was important. Many evenings Pops would take a few minutes to come to the pasture and watch Kevin play.

"Look Pops watching you," Barry told him the first evening Pops returned to the pasture.

"I know. He used to be a cricketer too," Kevin replied.

"So why he stop playing cricket?" Asked Jasper.

"He never told me, but Mr. Peters say that he get he foot break and had to stop," Kevin said.

This would explain why Pops walked with a limp. As long as Kevin could remember Pops always had a limp, and it never registered until Mr. Peters said that he had broken his foot. Kevin always thought that was just how his grandfather walked, so he never asked him.

Although Pops had a limp he was still fast and strong, therefore all the boys were afraid of him. He spoke with a deep voice and his dark, small eyes seemed mysterious, but when he was happy he would give such a smile that lit up the whole place. He was kind and was known as the village butcher. When people came to buy meat and they were short on money he would still give them the meat. People who sold food came from all over to buy his chickens and eggs, but they especially loved his pork and said that it tasted as if it had in sugar. Kevin looked forward to slaughtering days because he got the opportunity to kill an animal and would silently pretend that it was Big Bad Billy he was beating.

There was this one time after he cut the head off a chicken and it got away and flew all over the yard, spurting blood all about until it finally realized its head was off and dropped down dead.

Kevin particularly remembered the day they killed Benny the pig—that was a good day. They wrapped wire around two wooden clothes pins and pinned them onto Benny's ears while he was tied with a short rope to the side of the pen. Next they plugged the other end into a generator and electrocuted Benny. Kevin remembered that when Benny was alive he would often try to bite him when it was feeding time because he hated Kevin. One day Benny escaped from the pen and chased Kevin all over the yard, and his cousin had to capture Benny and replace him in the pen. So Kevin was glad when they killed Benny.

There was another man in the village who also kept animals, but his meat was never as good as Pops' and he eventually had to close down his business because of a lack of customers. Two days before he closed his business one of his cows fell in a well and broke all four of its legs, and some of the men in the village had to use ropes to lift it out. When they got the cow out they cut up the cow right there and shared out the beef to whoever wanted. Kevin ate beef for days.

"Boy all that beef you eating gine make you real strong," his grandfather had told him.

"I want to be strong. I plan to play cricket for the rest of my life," Kevin said.

"Well, as I says nobody can't stop you, just don't listen to their negative words, be like a duck." Pops said.

"A duck Pops?"

"Yes, the next time the rain fall I will show you what I mean."

A few days later it started raining. Kevin ran outside to the sheds and reminded his grandfather about the duck thing. His grandfather left off milking the cow and said to him:

"You see that duck there? Look at the water on its back."

"But Pops there is no water on the duck's back, all running off." Kevin replied.

"Good, that is what I mean when people tell you negative words, just let it roll off." Pops said and went back to milking Betsy.

Kevin stood watching the duck as he reflected on the many times he was told that he was wasting time playing cricket, and that he would never leave the village because he was poor and poor people didn't get far in life, only rich people did. He was aware of his reality, but in his heart he felt that life would turn in his favor. He did not know when, but he was certain of how—cricket was his ticket out and he was just waiting for that moment.

"You can't stop birds from flying over your head, but you can stop them from building a nest in your hair."

Pops said this to him as he realized that Kevin was still deep in thought. Pops always had a way of assuring Kevin that life was not always what it seemed, and that someday things would improve as long as he kept the right attitude.

"The right attitude determine your altitude." Pops would often say.

Growing up in an environment like this was healthy for Kevin, whose father was never around to affirm him. Pops cared for him as though he was his own son. Everything that he knew, he taught Kevin. He showed Kevin how to fix bicycles, how to fish, how to roast breadfruits, and when he was in the gully what fruits he should or shouldn't eat. Kevin was life to Pops, and Pops was life to Kevin.

Kevin learnt from early never to disrespect his grandfather. Although Pops was not constantly angry like Mother, Kevin had an encounter with him that left a permanent mark on the back of his leg where Pops gave him a lash with the same stick he would use to control the cows as he took them out to pasture. This was because Kevin thought he could interrupt Pops when he was speaking, so Pops lashed him while shouting:

"Don't interrupt me again!"

Kevin knew that although Pops loved him he could easily get rid of him, and no one would find him. He loved his grandfather, but there was a bridge that he dared not cross ever again.

"These young people today rude as hell." Pops was fretting one day in the easter vacation as he listened to a woman call in on the radio complaining that she couldn't control her nine year old son. Pops could not comprehend such madness and was furious to the point that he wanted to kick Betsy, but he remembered the last time he did so Betsy kicked down the milk bucket for two mornings straight. Instead, he said a few of his 'choice words'.

Kevin was just coming down the backyard steps when he heard Pops, but pretended that he did not hear and continued on his way to pick clamacherries to stick his newspaper kite which took just twenty minutes to make. Most of the boys in the village made their own kites, and if any boy did not have a kite it was best that he stayed home when they went to the pasture to fly them.

Kite season was a time to show creativity in making a kite, and the best looking or biggest kite won a prize of a pack of marbles, a roll of string, a toy car or anything which the promoters knew a little boy would want to play with.

7...Coming of Age

Not only was Kevin keen on playing cricket, but he also applied himself to learning his class work and although he never came first in class, he always gained a position among the top five students. Pops made it mandatory that after cricket on evenings Kevin did his homework, and under Pop's careful eye and the light of the lamp with the chimney which read 'Home Sweet Home', Kevin would sit and do his work while mother prepared dinner.

"Dem is want people who could read and write and not nuhbody who frighten to talk in front a camera, so wake up and finish this work," Pops would say to Kevin when he had fallen asleep while doing his homework.

At school Kevin's favorite subject was spelling

and Ms. Jameson his spelling teacher always had something nice to say to him after each spelling test.

"Mr. Bratts if you continue like this we might have to ask you to teach the class," or "Kevin you are a born leader."

The coach also encouraged him to be the best and Kevin never disappointed him, so that by the time Kevin was fourteen years old he was making his school cricket team proud. He was hitting big sixes and lashing fours across the pasture like a real professional. There was no longer a wish in heart to hit the ball like Timmy, because he was striking the ball with such force that Timmy was now in his shadow. Then one day Mr. Gilkes, the manager of the Under-20 cricket club, came to the school looking for the young man whom he heard was working wonders.

"If you want Kevin he is playing cricket on the pasture," Mr. Walcott told Mr. Gilkes as he enquired about him.

"Thank you sir," replied Mr. Gilkes.

Kevin was batting when he heard that 'some man' from a cricket club was asking for him, so he decided to show off his cricketing skills. The match was Red House against Green House. Kevin was the captain of the Green House team and was knocking every ball for six that George from the Red House team was bowling. He finally led his team to victory at eighty-nine runs not out.

Mr. Gilkes was amazed at how skillful Kevin was at cricket as he stood there watching the game. After the game he approached Kevin.

"Are you Kevin Bratts?"

"Yes Sir," replied Kevin.

"We are looking for all round cricketers to represent the Under-20 team. Do you think you have what it takes?"

"Yes Sir," answered Kevin.

"I see that you do," said Mr. Gilkes. "We will keep in touch."

"Thank you Sir," Kevin replied and hurried off to his class to do revision for his exams. Having completed his last set of exams he waited eagerly for the results and was elated to discover that he came second in class. He continued to play cricket for the school team until he finished school and led the school team to victory after victory.

When Kevin finished school he worked for Ms.

Peters cutting her lawn and walking her dogs because her husband was always too drunk to do anything. Kevin also worked a bit at the local horse stables as a groomer, yet he continued to play cricket even though he was tired most days. A few months after finishing school Kevin was chosen to represent Barbados as a batsman in the Under-20 cricket team. He was just sixteen years old, but he was fierce with the bat. Things were happening so fast that Kevin couldn't believe that it was true.

This would be the first time that Kevin would be playing on a pitch other than the school pitch and the big pasture. A sense of fear came over him, but he quickly shook it off. This was his big moment and he couldn't wait to tell Jan the good news. When he did she was sad that he would have to leave. The match was in Trinidad and she didn't have the money to go. The club was paying for Kevin and the other members.

"Don't worry Jan, I will be back before you can count to ten," Kevin said.

"But Trinidad is so far away," sulked Jan.

"The coach says it is just over there," Kevin said as he pointed over the cherry tree.

The day he was to leave he thought that Jan would cry, but to his surprise she hugged him and said:

"Go and bring back that medal."

This was the first time that Kevin was leaving Barbados and he was a little scared as he boarded the plane, but soon relaxed as the plane leveled off. When he arrived in Trinidad he only had a few days before his first match with the Under-20 Barbados cricket club called the Bat Team against a Trinidadian team called Fearless.

The day of the game, Kevin was the last man to bat. The Fearless team was winning the game, and the crowd loved it. There was one man left to bat before Kevin, but the coach came and said to him:

"We have to make six runs off one ball. Can you do it?"

Kevin was sitting there waiting for his chance and was wondering what it would be like on the big pitch. He knew that he would have to hit the ball harder than usual, because the outfield was way bigger than what he was accustomed to. So when the coach came to him he was ready. He stood up, looked up and onto the field and gave an affirming nod:

"Yes."

Kevin could feel the air rushing into his body as he took one long breath and walked out onto the field. He felt a chill run right down his spine, and then a peace came over him as he clenched the bat tighter. He knew that this was not an impossible task. The opposing team was being cheered on by the home crowd. They were confident that the game was already won.

Kevin walked onto the pitch, adjusted his pads and gloves, and took his stance. The crowd settled down as Nathan the fast bowler from the team Fearless got ready to bowl. He had already bowled out all the other members of Kevin's team, and he and the crowd were sure that dismissing Kevin would be an easy task.

Nathan took off running towards Kevin, and released the ball at top speed. Kevin braced himself, went down on one knee, and hit that ball so hard that it went high and far for six. When the crowd saw the play and the sky-high ball they went silent. The whole stadium could not believe what they had just seen. Nathan was speechless as he walked over to Kevin and shook his hand, and the whole stadium applauded. Kevin's play made him the man of the match, and created that day the best six ever so far by any team which batted against the Fearless team.

"Wow, Kevin that's the best six ever," Johnson from his team said as he gave Kevin a slap on the back.

"That's it. You are what we need," said the coach.

"Good job."

"Excellent play," said another fellow whom Kevin did not know.

The game was broadcast live so all those who were interested in hearing or seeing Kevin play were not disappointed. When Kevin returned to Barbados he was greeted at the airport by friends and family as they congratulated him on doing such an excellent job. Pops was all smiles and gave him a big hug at home and said:

"Boy eating all that beef really paying off!"

Mother was in the kitchen and as soon as Kevin came through the back door she smiled at him and said:

"Well done." This was a moment he would never forget.

After that game Kevin was elevated to first man and after a few games was made captain. Match after match Kevin took his team to victory nationally and across the Caribbean. There was not one game that the team lost and it was hard to ignore that it was all because of Kevin. He literally turned the team around as he taught them new ways to attack the ball and stay focused on the task at hand.

He was becoming somebody important and famous, and he loved it. Kevin was getting better and better by the second. He had developed his own style of batting that a few tried to copy, but failed. Cricket took Kevin all around the Caribbean and by the time he was twenty years old and chosen for the West Indies Team, he was traveling all around the world. He was visiting places that he never knew existed. His face was all over the news and in the newspaper as he played the game he was born for and loved more than anything else.

The lessons he learnt at school from the cricket coach had served him well and although that chapter of his school life was over, a new chapter of being an adult had begun. Kevin was gaining popularity, yet he still helped Pops with the animals and filled the barrel every day with water from the local standpipe until the time when he surprised Pops and mother with enough money to repair the house and install water and electricity. The day the carpenters and masons came to build over the house Kevin was there and over the following months if he was not playing cricket he helped the workmen in whatever way possible. Finally the construction was completed, and the days of long trips to the pipe and to the shop to buy kerosene oil were over.

"Your mother and I were talking and we want to thank you for what you did," Pops said to Kevin as he played with his dogs in the yard. Pops had a way of speaking perfect English when he wanted to, or just Bajan when he didn't want to make the effort. Kevin knew that what Pops said was really coming from deep within because he formed each word perfectly.

As the money began to accumulate again after repairing Mother's house, Kevin finally had enough money to invite Jan to some of the games and she was happy to be with him. By this time her father had grown really fond of Kevin and therefore allowed her to travel with him.

Jan was there to encourage Kevin when he became frustrated or annoyed about something. She felt it was her responsibility to look after him and she surely did. Kevin was reaping joy everywhere he went. He had his cricket and his girl.

Pops was always talking about Kevin and always had his old gold star radio set to sports news. Mother too was very proud of Kevin, although she was not much for showing emotion. Kevin knew that she was happy for him because every time he and Jan returned from a match she would just say "My boy" with a big smile.

Mother started to commend him more by saying things like "good job" or "I am proud of you." Over the years she had somehow softened to him and did not appear as angry as before. She did not say much to Jan, but she was never mean to her and would always offer a welcoming smile. What more could Jan ask for anyway? Mother was now warming up to her own son after so many years. Kevin did not say much to her either, but they both knew that they loved each other in a strange kind of way.

Many things were changing in Kevin's life. His world was evolving to become what he had always dreamt and spoken of, and because of this some of his childhood friends became jealous of him. Bruce was the first to distance himself because Kevin told him that he could not take him to a particular cricket match. However, Barry was his constant friend. If there was one friend Kevin could rely upon it was him.

After the incident on the big pasture with Ms. Prescott and Big Bad Billy, Barry lost interest in cricket and developed a love for mechanics and cars after his parents bought an old Peugeot from Matthias' parents. Barry could tell from ten feet away what part a car needed. When Mr. Johnson, Matthias or his parents' cars needed fixing they would all come to Barry. Barry did not go to school to learn mechanics; it was something he was born with. It was amazing to watch him pick down a whole engine, detect the problem, reassemble it and cause that car to sound just like a brand new car.

Kevin had gained many new friends as a member of the West Indies Cricket team and was always on tour throughout the Caribbean and wider world. On one of these tours in Jamaica, while buying some fruits and vegetables in the market after one of his cricket matches, he felt a tap on his shoulder and a voice said:

"Is that you Kevin? The best cricketer?"

Kevin turned around ready to be greeted by an adoring fan and bumped into Billy. Kevin's heart almost fell out as fear gripped him like a bench vice. Even after all this time he still had an unconscious fear of Billy. Immediately his mind raced back to their last encounter and he was sure that Billy would have his revenge. He wanted to run, but the market was full and Billy had him cornered. To his amazement, Billy held out his hand and said:

"Hello Kevin."

Reluctantly, Kevin held out his hand and said: "Hello Billy."

"I won't hurt you here, there are too many people around. Just joking. You don't have to be afraid, I have left that life behind."

Billy told Kevin that he was living in Jamaica and playing football for a Jamaican team. He and his father couldn't get along anymore. Not that they were ever pals in the first place, so he eventually left the village and his old ways behind. Kevin remembered that day Billy and his father had had a big argument and Billy left the house and village.

Now, looking at him, Kevin could not believe that this was the same Billy that terrorized him when he was a small boy. Billy had gotten bigger and he spoke in such a manner that demonstrated that he had indeed matured.

"I can't believe that you are playing football," Kevin said to Billy.

"Not only you. After I left the village I was into fishing. Then one day I saw an advertisement in the papers for men who wanted to learn football, and as they say, the rest is history. Let's have a drink."

At the bar they talked about old times and settled their conflict over a couple of beers and some good laughter.

"Nuh matter where you go yuh does find a Bajan."

"Wha you gossiping 'bout now Suzie?" Evon asked.

"Me cousin tell me he see Kevin and Billy drinking Rum together in Jamaica," Suzie replied.

No one living in the village would have imagined that this was possible until one day they saw them talking to each other after Billy came back home to visit his sick father. Then the villagers started a saying: "The lion and the lamb are friends."

Kevin was becoming influential. He was a man now and he felt it was time to move away from home permanently and get on with his new life.

The old neighborhood could not hold him down; his dreams were too big and he had to live them out. He had travelled to so many places and there was so much more he wanted to see. He had transitioned from a boy bringing water from the local standpipe, doing homework from the light of the kerosene lamp and eating food cooked on the outside stove to a man with a mission.

Although she never said it, Mother certainly did not want him to leave. She did not mind so much his travelling back and forth, but to leave for good was something her heart was not prepared for. Although she knew that it would happen someday, she just could not bridge the gap between her mind and her heart.

Kevin understood her pain, but it was his time to shine and he was determined that he would do what he wanted to do without any restrictions. The dreaded day for Mother came when he said goodbye to her and he and Jan left with great joy and anticipation about their bright future together living in Trinidad.

Pops wanted to cry, but he felt confident that he had invested enough time and effort into preparing Kevin for this moment. This was not his grandson he was saying goodbye to, but his son. All that he knew he had taught Kevin. As Kevin was about to leave, Pops said to him: "Wait a minute son. I have something for you."

Pops went to the sheds and returned with a small leather bag and said:

"I made this from some of the sheep skin; whenever you smell this remember where you came from."

Kevin hugged Pops and said: "I will never forget."

Mother's sad heart sank to her belly as she watched Kevin walk away. Pops stood there watching and just smiled and said to Kevin.

"Just be careful son."

Pops returned to the comfort of the shed and wept because he would no longer have Kevin around to talk to or help him with the animals. His life would never be the same without Kevin. His animals brought him joy, but they could never replace his grandson. Mother and Uncle Frank, his two children, could not even satisfy the longing for companionship he knew he would have with Kevin's absence.

Tears welled up too in his mothers' eyes, but

only after he left. Kevin said his goodbyes and held Jan's hand and walked to the taxi. They drove off into their future as a couple.

9...Famous Boy

Besides playing cricket for the West Indies, Kevin also played for a local team in Trinidad. On that team there was a batsman whom Kevin admired and silently hoped that the captain would pair them up one day. Much to his delight, that day came quicker than he anticipated and Kevin opened batting with one of the greatest cricketers he knew. This provided Kevin the highlight of his life. That day they scored 250 runs not out, and won the game with two wickets in hand. The crowd went wild and had to be restrained from rushing onto the field. That game was by far the most exciting moment of his career, as he got to show off his skill with one of the best in the game.

That pushed Kevin a bar up and now he was

sure that his name would be going down in the books as one of the better cricketers.

What more could he ask for? He used to be just a local boy from humble beginnings, but now he was a star player. Kevin could not believe it; this was the most exciting time of his entire life. He was soaring; not like a pigeon, but like an eagle. His head was high in the clouds and there was no sign of him coming back down. He was a top player now, having achieved what so many youngsters wished they had achieved. He was proud, just like a peacock, and he had no problem showing his pretty feathers.

He was getting calls from many cricket managers from all around the world to come and play for them, but he was committed to the West Indies Cricket Team. Commitment was a lesson he had learnt from an early age.

"When you have committed yourself to a thing always stick it out to the end," Pops would always say.

The West Indies Cricket Team was winning match after match with Kevin as its captain. So much so that by the time Kevin was twenty-five years old he had already made a name for himself. While he was still living in Trinidad many aspiring young cricketers were seeking him out for advice and to know his secret to success, but his answer was always the same.

"Apply yourself and you shall do well; never limit yourself."

Whenever cricket was being played, Barbadians would be glued to the television or radio to see or hear their local boy Kevin hitting those sixes and fours, or bowling out the opposing team, because he was not only a great batsman, but also an excellent fast bowler.

Many would say "That's my boy" or "That's my son." Somehow he had become everyone's family. He was a hero to many, a star boy to others, but an inspiration to all. To those who really knew him well, he was still Kevie.

He and Jan also started an apartment rental business and were having as much success with that as with cricket. Kevin was no fool; he knew how to invest and make his money grow.

He was making so much money that he was able to send some back to Mother and have a bigger and better house built for her. He and Jan bought a really nice house, but he hardly spent time at home, as he was always on the move. If he was not playing cricket he was promoting it, with advertisements on the television and radio.

Together he and Jan were a real team and they were happy. Money was always around and they were just floating through life.

Cricket had turned a 'nobody' into a 'somebody' and Kevin was a success whenever he touched the bat or ball. People knew that no team could stand a chance against the West Indies Team once Kevin was playing, and no team did.

Once it was announced that the West Indies Team was playing in a match or series the men at the gambling post were ready to bet. The voices were clear and the decisions unanimous:

"I know who I betting on."

"For sure Kevin is the Captain."

"Them can't lose, them is de champions."

The ones who were against the West Indies team were few, and they would always lose their money when they bet against the team. In Barbados many arguments would occur at Evon's rum shop over disputes about whether Kevin was getting too old for cricket.

"You see how he running? He look old to you?"

said Peters.

"De man fast like a bullet," Evon replied.

"He still running like he is twenty," old man George would say.

Uncle Frank would just sit in the corner sipping his rum and would not say a word to defend his nephew's honor. As far as he was concerned, cricket was a waste of time.

Then one day Kevin and Jan surprised the men at the rum shop and turned up for a drink on one of his visits to Barbados to see his family.

"Look who come down by we!" Evon shouted.

Uncle Frank looked up and back down to his glass.

"De best cricketer in the whole world." Old man George said and went back to sleep. He was too drunk to keep his eyes open.

Kevin visited Mother and Pops whenever he got the chance and was true to his promise to Pops that he would never forget where he came from and how it all started. Coming home was always a breath of fresh air, because he got the opportunity to relax and spend some time at the beach with some of his old buddies who were still in living in Barbados.

"Barry you look like an old bat and smell like a tub of grease," Kevin teased Barry who had never left Barbados or the village.

"When is the last day you look in a mirror?" Barry would respond.

Many times Kevin had invited Barry down to stay with them, but Barry refused.

"If God wanted me to fly, I would've been born with wings."

Barry was afraid of travelling on an airplane, but he always made Kevin's time back home enjoyable and drove him everywhere he wanted to go. Returning to Barbados was also a time for Jan to visit her parents and spend some time with Pedro her father.

"Jan are you still attending church?" He would often ask.

"Yes Daddy," she would reply.

Since residing in Trinidad Jan attended church only once, because most Sundays she was at cricket matches or at home. She hated lying to her father, but it was easier that way because she knew that if she told him the truth that he would stop speaking to her, just like the time he asked her to sing at a function at church and she refused, and Pedro did not say another word to her for the rest of her vacation.

Living in Trinidad was a great experience for them, but Kevin had always wanted to live in New York, so they sold their house, cars and apartment rental business, and moved to America after spending five years in Trinidad. It was an easy transition for them.

10...Caught

As a successful cricketer and businessman, Kevin was often invited to a party or some special occasion, so it was not in any way strange when a prominent man in the cricket industry invited Kevin and Jan to a special celebration in honor of his son who scored four sixes in one over and led the team to victory. At his son's request Kevin was asked to share his journey from a boy who loved cricket to the successful man he was.

However, Jan could not attend because she was not feeling well, so Kevin went alone. After his speech Kevin sat at a bar across the street from the celebration having a few drinks with some of the men. From the corner of his eye he saw a woman approach the bar and he heard her ask the bartender for a drink.

"Hi Harry... hit me wid a cold one."

Kevin immediately recognized the voice and turned in her direction.

"I can't believe it. Veronica St. Clair is that really you all the way from Barbados?" Kevin asked.

The woman looked up from her drink, startled that someone other than Harry knew her name and where she originated, and responded with a huge smile when she realized who it was that called her name.

"Kevin? I have not seen you in years. How are you and what have you been up to?"

"I am great."

After talking about life, school days and growing up in the village, Veronica asked: "Have you see Jan Matthews lately?"

"Lately? Jan is my girl and she was always my only girl since school days."

"Are you serious?" Veronica almost dropped her glass as she continued. "You and Jan still together after all these years?"

"Yes! And that's how it will be forever," Kevin said.

"You never had another besides Jan?" Veronica asked in disbelief.

Kevin ignored the question and started talking about his success in cricket and was so totally wrapped up in the conversation that he was not aware of the time.

"Oh shoot. I got to call Jan…. Hello honey, sorry I didn't call earlier," Kevin said as Jan answered the phone.

For the next ten minutes they continued whispering 'sweet nothings', as the old people would say.

"I will call when I am leaving," Kevin told Jan and sent a kiss over the phone.

After reassuring her that he would be home as soon as possible, he resumed conservation with Veronica, who was still at the bar sipping her drink. She told him all about her new house and the lovely swimming pool she had installed only a week earlier. After a few more drinks she asked:

"You want to see my place? It is not far from here."

"Why do you want me to see your house?" he asked jokingly.

"I think you would like it," she replied.

Feeling a little weary and tipsy, he agreed and

they left the function. Veronica led the way in her sports car and Kevin followed closely behind. When they arrived at the house, he was the first to speak.

"Wow… this is a lovely house."

"You must see it when outside is really bright. Come and go inside."

Veronica was one of Jan's good friends when they were children and she never cared too much about anything, therefore Kevin was impressed to see how much she had achieved and how confidently she spoke as she led the way into the house. Kevin looked around, fascinated by the many pictures which adorned the walls and the scent of vanilla oil radiating throughout the living room.

"Would you like a drink?" she offered.

"What do you have?" Kevin asked.

"The wine is in the fridge. Help yourself," she suggested as she disappeared around the corner.

Kevin found the wine and poured himself a drink.

"This is a really nice house," he whispered as he sipped his wine while listening to Veronica humming a tune in the shower.

"I will be there soon," she shouted from the bedroom as she searched for something to wear.

When she returned she was wearing a long black dress revealing all the curves of her body.

"Do you like this?" she asked him. "I had to get comfortable."

"It is nice," he said trying his best not look at the dress.

This was the first woman besides Jan that he had gotten this close to. His first instinct was to leave, but against his better judgment and with the alcohol flowing through his blood stream and Veronica's body staring at him through the dress, he decided to stay.

"Do you want to go by the pool?" Veronica asked Kevin, who by this time was taking longer looks at the dress. Veronica noticed this, but said nothing.

"Why not?" he replied, as he watched her lead the way.

At the poolside Kevin sat away from Veronica as she continued to speak about the cost of the building the house, how the workmen tried to rob her and all the challenges she encountered while building it, but Kevin did not hear one word; his mind was focused on the dress and what was under it.

"Why don't you come and sit next to me?" she asked in her most sensual voice.

"That might not be such a good idea," he replied and remained where he was.

"Nothing will happen between us… you are my good friend," she said as she walked over and sat next to him, placing her hand on his leg.

Kevin got up and said:

"This is getting weird, thanks for the drink… and you do have a lovely house."

Kevin got into his car and drove home. Jan heard the car as it pulled into the driveway and because she was feeling better and was anticipating his arrival, met him at the door.

"Hi hon, Phew. Hon you have been drinking."

"Just a few drinks with the boys."

He wanted to mention that he saw Veronica, but he decided not to. That night as he lay in bed he kept thinking about her and went to sleep hoping that he would see her soon. That hope became a reality one week later when he saw her at short video presentation in which he was demonstrating the correct way to hold a bat and how to be always vigilant when on field. She was a special quest invited by a friend of the camera man.

"We have met again. Ain't that a coincidence?"

"Yes we have," he replied.

"So now that's over what are your plans?" she asked.

"Nothing much. The shoot finished early so I got some time to burn."

"Okay. Outside is really bright… do you still want to see the beauty of my house?" Veronica asked.

"Yeah, okay," he responded and followed her to the house.

"I see what you mean, the house does look great," Kevin said when they were finally at the house.

"I told you so," she agreed.

Kevin stood looking up at the beautiful design of the overhung roof and was so impressed that he was not aware that Veronica had drawn closer to him until he felt her hand on his shoulder and her dress sleeve rubbing his hand with each gust of wind. As she gently pressed her body to his, he knew that this was not good idea. Yet he loved the sensations. However, he fought against the urges and said.

"Veronica, we can't. I am with Jan."

"It's alright, nothing will happen, we can just sit together," she reassured him and encouraged him to sit next to her again.

Like a sheep about to be caught, he agreed and sat next to her. Unlike Kevin, she was an expert at seduction, and with Kevin being the novice he was, Veronica weaved her web around him that day. Although they did not have sex, she had already teased his desire for her with just one kiss. After that first experience with her, Kevin was trapped. Many evenings after that he lied to Jan that he and the boys were having a few drinks just so he could go and spend time with Veronica.

It was on one of those occasions as they sat by the poolside having a drink that she offered him some marijuana.

"What is this?" Kevin asked.

"Just something to help us have some more fun," she replied.

Kevin had seen marijuana once before when the coach was warning them about the dangers of drugs. "Drugs and sports don't mix." The coach would often say.

"You need some of this. Try it." Veronica insisted while pressing her appealing body against his.

Although he knew about its danger, Kevin wanted to please Veronica. So he said:

"Yes. I will try it."

"Wow, I like this," he said as he took his first pull.

That night was the first time he used drugs and it was also the first time that he eventually gave in to Veronica's passion and had sex with her. Now he was really trapped; he had resisted long enough and like a struggling spider trying to be freed of the web around it, had given up fighting and was at Veronica's mercy, of which there was none.

11...The Fight

Little by little Jan was seeing less of Kevin as he spent more time at Veronica's house. Every day Kevin came up with some new excuse about why he was coming home late or why he needed to leave home. Jan never suspected that he was having an affair with another woman. She was sure that Kevin was at work or with the boys as he said, and she believed him until one day she received a call.

"Jan this is Sabrina, you would never believe who I saw yesterday?"

"Tell me," Jan replied anxiously.

"Veronica," Sabrina answered.

"Wow. Where? I have not seen her in years," Jan said excitedly.

"Don't be so excited because Kevin was with

her coming from a house on Fifth Avenue."

"Nah. Kevin was with his friends."

"Sorry Jan, but it was him," Sabrina said sorrowfully and put the phone down.

Jan fell to the bed weeping. She had trusted Kevin but now she felt used. She had to find out if this was true, so she regained posture and drove to Fifth Avenue to the house that Sabrina described. She knocked on the door and when Veronica opened it she confronted her, and they had a terrible argument.

"You mean it is you that stealing my man?" shouted Jan.

"Your man can think for himself and he chose me," replied Veronica.

"If you were doing something right he would not come by me."

"Well you can keep him. I should have known every sense that you dangerous and back stabbing," replied Jan.

Later that evening, as soon as Kevin entered the driveway, Jan was ready. She confronted him even before he got out of the car.

"Veronica? You are cheating on me with her?"

Kevin was speechless and shocked, because

this was the first time he had ever seen her this angry, and he was also afraid because she had a knife in her hand and was waving it in his face.

"I will cut your mouth off if you say one word," she continued.

Kevin sat in the car quietly as Jan continued.

"How many times have you done this to me?"

Then she ran off crying into the house. She slammed the bedroom door and refused to open it when Kevin knocked. There were no words Kevin could say to gain her forgiveness.

Even after all this confrontation, Jan still stayed with Kevin. She wanted so much to leave, but the shame and embarrassment of leaving was greater than the pain and betrayal she was experiencing. So she swallowed the grief and continued. But her trust in him was severed and she hated him for what he did to her.

Kevin wanted to stop using drugs and fooling around with Veronica. He realized the pain he was causing Jan and made a real effort to change his ways because he really did love her, so he announced to Veronica one day that he was going to end the relationship.

"We have to end this. I love Jan."

"I can't believe you are leaving all of this to go back to boring Jan?" Veronica screamed as she slapped Kevin in his face.

"I love Jan and I am tired of hurting her." Kevin turned and walked away.

"Well don't come back!" she shouted.

Kevin got into his car and headed for home, thinking all the way what he would say to Jan. As he drove into the driveway his thoughts were still all over the place. When he entered the house Jan was surprised to see him, but said nothing. Kevin spoke first. "I done with Veronica and I am so sorry for hurting you."

"How could you do this to me?" Jan asked.

"I made a horrible mistake, and I am sorry." He pleaded.

Kevin continued to apologize profusely.

Eventually after three weeks and two days of begging for her forgiveness, Jan finally forgave him and over time she became excited because she had her man back all for herself. They started going out together again as her trust level in him elevated. Things were back to normal. Kevin was playing cricket and returning home early.

If there were meetings that needed his attention and presence he hurried home as soon as they were over. He stopped hanging out with some of his old drinking buddies, and he was spending every free moment with Jan.

But deep in Kevin was an urge. He had tried really hard and had made it up to two months without using drugs and visiting Veronica. Then one afternoon he saw her at the supermarket.

"So you back with your woman and done with me?" She asked as she greeted Kevin.

"You know I love Jan and I don't want to hurt her anymore," Kevin replied.

"Cool, cool. But when you get bored and want some excitement call me. In fact just come by, you know where the house is," Veronica said and walked off swirling her butt. She knew that Kevin was watching her and she smiled to herself thinking: *He will be back. He can't refuse me.*

Kevin tried for days to get Veronica's voice and offer from his head, but most of all he could not get her body off his mind. Seeing her again brought back the memories of their times together and he wanted her. He wanted everything that she offered—the sex and the drugs. He battled for weeks with these thoughts and images. Not even Jan knew. She was just glad to have Kevin back. She was starting to trust him again and believed again in their dream. Then one evening Jan came home not talking. She had seen some of her girlfriends at the shoe store and they were telling her about Kevin.

"You sure Kevin is finished with Veronica? Cause I see them talking in the supermarket and he hug she up." Sabrina said.

"And I see how he look at she. He ain't even see me over by the dairy section," added Angela.

Sabrina and Angela were Jan's friends from Barbados. Jan had reunited with them a few years earlier while shopping. They loved to gossip and Jan knew this, but she could not stop thinking about what Sabrina said and it was making her angry. When she got home Kevin greeted her as usual and she started to vent her rage.

"I thought you said that you will never see that female dog again?"

"Who and what are you talking about?" asked Kevin calmly.

"You know! And you gone back sleeping with her." Jan said.

"What the hell are you talking about Jan?" Kevin asked, as he too was getting mad.

"I ain't even calling she name, but you is a dog just like she!" shouted Jan.

"Look… I leaving in here 'cause you gone crazy, accusing me of something I ain't do."

"Well, if you leave don't expect to see me when you return!" Jan shouted after Kevin who was already on his way out.

Kevin slammed the door, got in his car and drove off. He could not believe that all this time he was trying hard to do the right thing and ignore Veronica, yet this just happened and he was getting angrier and angrier by the second the more he thought about Jan accusing him of something he was not doing.

"She is accusing me? Well I am going to do it for real."

Kevin drove straight to Veronica's house. She greeted him at the door with a sensual kiss and asked:

"What took you so long, Sugar?"

Kevin and Veronica spent that night together drinking, smoking, and having sex. Kevin felt guilty as he drove home with a splitting headache the following morning.

"Where you went?" Jan asked Kevin as soon as he opened the door.

Kevin was in no mood for talking, so he headed straight to bed. Jan stood in disbelief. She wondered where he went the night before, yet in the back of her mind she knew that he was at Veronica's house. The thought was making her sick to her stomach and she headed to the bedroom. Kevin was already asleep. As she stood looking down at him a million ideas flooded her thoughts on how to kill him. The love she had for him was replaced by a strong hatred and she wanted to end it all. Only a few months earlier he had apologized and she took him back. He had promised then that he would not see Veronica again, but he lied and she felt betrayed and worthless. "What does she have that I don't?" Jan asked one of her girlfriends when she called her on the phone.

"It's not you. Don't blame yourself," her girlfriend said.

However, Jan still felt it was her fault because she was the one that took him back and she replied:

"I should have known that he won't change. If my father was alive Kevin would be a dead man today."

Pedro, Jan's father, had died three years before all of this, but when he was alive he always maintained that if Kevin was to ever hurt his baby he would kill him. He was a diabetic and had gone into a diabetic coma after he consumed too many ripe mangoes. Jan had cried her heart out when she heard the news about her father's death, but she was away with Kevin at a cricket match. When she thought of the sacrifices she made for Kevin, there was only one thing left to do.

Kevin woke up the next morning with a terrible hangover. When he opened his eyes Jan was standing over him with a knife.

"You know I here thinking about cutting your throat? After all I do for you, I even missed my father's funeral for you and you sleeping with a slut?"

"Go ahead Jan, do it," he ordered.

But she could not harm Kevin, so she dropped the knife and walked away. Kevin got up, bathed and left the house. Jan stood by the window and watched him as he drove off and disappeared around the corner. She knew he was going straight to Veronica's house.

As the tears rolled down her face she remembered the days when they were so in love that nothing could separate them. But this was happening and she didn't know how to stop it. She wanted so much to run after him and beg him to stay, but she knew that it was a waste of time and effort, for the Kevin that she loved was gone and replaced by some kind of monster that was terrifying, both in her sleeping and waking moments.

Though Kevin never hit Jan, what she was experiencing was worse than any beating she could imagine. This pain was tearing her from the inside and she felt powerless to stop the effects. If only she could have seen the future, she would never have gone to that swamp, and she would never have introduced herself to him.

Her life was a disaster. She had given up on her dreams to be a singer to help him build his. She had put her life on hold and was living his life, and now she felt so empty and lost. The thought of committing suicide was on her mind, but with every last strength she had within her she resisted. For some reason beyond her understanding, she wanted to live.

As Kevin turned into Veronica's driveway and stopped the car, he looked at his hands which were shaking. His head felt dizzy at the thought that Jan could have killed him. He quickly forgot that near-killing experience as he saw Veronica standing by the door. He was hooked on drugs and Veronica like a hose to a pipe. During the following weeks he hardly went home and when he did, he and Jan never spoke. She felt guilty for pushing him away and he felt sorry for what he was doing to her, but the pleasure from Veronica and the drugs was too satisfying for him to consider Jan.

Jan was trapped in a cage of hopelessness and every day she felt like the four walls of the house were closing in on her. She was too ashamed to call her mother and dreaded the night that was on the way. Nighttime was always the most fearful and longest period ever, for this was the time when the demons tormented her soul. Depression was her daily portion and heartbreak was a constant pain. Why did her life turn out this way? She could not answer.

Her parents had a perfect marriage and she therefore felt that she and Kevin would have a great relationship as long as she did what she saw her mother do, which was to support her husband and care for him. In all of her life growing up she never heard her father say one angry word to her mother and her mother adored Pedro. Pedro's food was always ready and on the table when he came home from work, and when he was finished eating she would massage his legs because he had poor blood circulation. Jan's parents had been married for over thirty years, and in that time Pedro never cheated on her mother Shirley. Jan knew this because she had asked him a few years back.

"Daddy you ever cheated on Mummy?"

"No sweetheart, and I never will. There is no need, your mother is enough for me," he replied.

Jan's expectations were high and it made the disappointment even greater. She wanted to leave Kevin, but she felt pulled in so many directions. Where was the dedicated and committed man she fell head over heels for? The man that made her smile and laugh until her belly ached? Now all that ached her was the pain he was causing her and not even her friends could ease that hurt with their suggestions to go out.

"Jan there is a nice picture showing. Let's go and see it," Angela suggested.

"I don't have the time or energy," Jan replied.

The house was her prison. There were no bars, yet she could not go outside. Even the air smelled stale and there was always a bad taste in her mouth. There was nothing that brought her comfort. She wanted to move on, but she couldn't. She wanted to forget about Kevin, but she couldn't. She wanted to kill Kevin, but she couldn't. It seemed that nothing she wanted to do, whether good or bad, was within her power, so she opted for imprisonment within her own house.

While she lived in fear, Kevin was enjoying life. Nothing seemed to bother him. His desires were being met and every day was a chance to explore some new adventure. He was so much on a pleasure trip that he ignored his calls from Pops and Mother. He distanced himself from everything which reminded him of Jan, and which would force him to accountability.

Months passed on and his family heard not a word from Kevin.

"Pops, Kevin call you recently?" Mother asked.

"If he did, don't you think I would say so?"

It was just a matter of time before they became so frustrated trying to reach Kevin that they stopped calling.

Veronica's web of deception and seduction was around Kevin's neck like an anaconda on its prey, and she controlled his every move. He was a slave to her desires and fantasies. One Sunday evening while he was at her house she went into the bedroom and returned with a black box and placed it on the table, then she took out a vial of white powder and said to him:

"Kevin, have some of this."

"What is this?"

She laughed and replied: "This is cocaine."

"Why not? Can't be that bad."

That was the first of the many times that he used cocaine, and he was addicted to its taste and effects. Consequences and penalties were not on his mind as he became a regular user.

"What would coach say if he knew we are using

drugs?" His friend who played cricket with him asked.

"He will never know, because we are not addicted," Kevin replied.

But Kevin was addicted, and slowly it wrapped itself around his cold heart, forcing out the last bit of love he had for Jan.

Veronica had succeeded at her plan and he was her prisoner to do all she required of him.

"Hey sugar, this is what we call life and happiness." Veronica stated as they lay on her bed.

"Yeah…" Kevin replied with silly grin on his face.

12...From Fame to Failure

Kevin was on a high, literally. He was using drugs daily, which was easy since Veronica was his supplier, but he was still able to play great cricket and his habit went unnoticed by his fans and superiors. However, this deception was not hidden from the coach and he questioned Kevin directly.

"Are you using drugs?"

"No," Kevin lied, but the coach was persistent and eventually Kevin only admitted to using marijuana.

"This is the first warning from me. If you use again I am taking this matter to the board."

Kevin heard the coach, but he was caught up in all the pleasures that were offered to him because money was no longer an issue. He had lots of it. He was spending it on clothes, driving the best cars, living in the best houses, eating at the best hotels and wearing the most expensive jewelry. He had lots of friends too, so every day after work there was a party.

Kevin was not only using drugs, but he was also distributing cocaine for Veronica and was making tons of money. Eventually he started using the cocaine he was supposed to be distributing, which reduced the profits she expected.

"Kevin what happen to the money?" Veronica asked him.

He lied and said, "Sales were a little slow."

Veronica soon discovered what he was doing and therefore she and her clients could no longer trust him.

"Look Kevin, you are my boy, but you using up my stuff." Veronica said.

"Your stuff? You mean we stuff." He blurted out.

"My people want you out… so this is where we part!!" Veronica shouted.

"Just so Veronica? You are kicking me out?" Kevin shouted back at her.

"Yes."

Veronica was a business woman and money was more important to her than Kevin was. So just like that Kevin was out of a supplier and he was desperate for a fix. He searched around frantically and was able to hook up with a supplier called Shady-Shade, but his demanded price was high. Kevin didn't mind, because he had the money. Cost was not relevant because he needed to have his daily dosage of cocaine and he had been barely surviving with cigarettes and marijuana.

"They tell me that you got some good stuff." Kevin said to Shady-Shade as he was introduced to him by one of his drinking buddies.

"If you got the dough then I got the blow."

"I have the money. Now hit me with your best stuff."

By this time Kevin's career was over. He had ignored the pleas of the coach, and the board could no longer ignore the fact that their star player was not performing and thus the team was losing a few matches. The coach even offered to pay for his rehabilitation, but Kevin refused, stating: "I don't need no help." But in his heart he was shouting for help, but he was too proud to admit it then.

It was just a matter of time before Kevin used up all of his money, so in his desperation he started selling off his jewellery, then his cars and houses; anything to get money to continue his drug habit. Blinded by his addiction, he could not see that Shady-Shade was gaining all that he was losing. Every day he was making another man rich by the things he and Jan had worked so hard to accomplish. Everything he had worked so hard to gain he sold off just to get a fix.

One day he came to Jan demanding money.

"You can't have the apartment rental business or its money," Jan told him.

After Veronica had kicked Kevin out he was too ashamed to return to the house he and Jan shared, so he stayed in one of the apartments. Jan never went by the apartments, but she had a friend who was collecting the rent money for her because she never wanted to see Kevin. Her friend had mentioned to her before how bad Kevin looked.

When Jan saw him that day her heart almost broke her chest and fell out. By this time he was thirty-five years old and was so hooked on drugs that he had reached a stage that most people were surprised to know and see what had become of him. He could no longer hide his addiction and was almost unrecognizable. He had lost so much weight and size. Shady-Shade had taken everything and moved on. All the friends that Kevin had accumulated when money was flowing were now gone, and so were the girls.

Throughout all of this Jan was still hoping for a change. Her friends were begging her to leave Kevin, so with a broken heart, Jan was the last to leave. Having seen him that day made her decision easier. She could not handle what had become of the Kevin she loved. She had held on long enough hoping for a change, but there was none. In fact, it had gotten worse. She too had lost much weight crying night after night and refusing to eat. It pained her so much that she felt it in her bones. She could not have imagined that her true love would be a thorn in her side.

Many times she would think of going back home, but this time her thoughts became actions, so she sold their apartment business, the house and car that she was determined Kevin could not touch, and headed back home to her old village in Barbados. She was too broken to think about what her mother would say to her, or anyone else for that matter. Shame was the last thing on her mind. She needed help and although her mother would give her a good rebuke, she knew that it was all in love.

"Jan is coming, she is coming!" Her cousin Mary shouted.

As Jan got out of the taxi and descended the small hill to her mother's house she was glad that her father was not alive to see her like this. The peaceful Jan who left all those years ago was now replaced by a weary, worried and sad person. When her mother saw her the first words she said were:

"Jan why didn't you come back home or tell me what was going on? How could you keep this hidden from us?"

Jan was expecting something like this, so she simply replied: "Mummy you are right. I should've been back here years ago."

Jan submitted herself to being cared for by her mother and cousins, and over time she regained some measure of stability and assurance that all would be well. Kevin was no longer in her life and the need for him was gone. She had suffered at his hands for a long time, and yet every now and then she would think of him and wondered if he was still alive.

By this time Kevin had been kicked out of the cricket team long ago. He could no longer play cricket because of his drug addiction which had taken full control of his life. He had sold everything he had to support his habit and had become a shadow of what he used to be. The new owners of the apartments evicted Kevin, forcing him to be homeless. He was so addicted to drugs that he was begging on the streets for money to get his next high.

As he walked around town begging for money he was spat at and cursed. Finding shelter was hard, so he slept anywhere he could and ate any food that was discarded or given to him.

"We don't want any crack heads here," one store owner said as he kicked Kevin to the sidewalk.

Kevin was in too much pain and too hungry to respond, so he sat in the gutter and held out his hands to people as they passed by. Daily he sat begging and occasionally he would be pitied and given a bit more food than usual, and this extra food is what allowed him to live another day.

There were days when he ate nothing and days that he had just a little food. There were days that he could not get a fix and some days he would, because a drug lord called Stormy would give him some free cocaine, food and a place to sleep. Kevin had met him years ago when he was at the top of his game and had done a few 'drops' for him, but now it was impossible to do so, as he was just a skeleton of what he used to be and barely able to walk because of a sprained ankle he got running from some dogs. Although Stormy gave Kevin food, he would still offer him some money to buy food:

"Kevin I remember you were good to me when you had money, so here, hold this money."

"Thanks Stormy. I want to change but it real hard." Kevin confided in him.

People saw Kevin as just an addict and never took any interest in engaging him in conversation, but if they did they would realize that Kevin was intelligent, but he was lost and needed help.

Stormy was his only friend and Kevin shared many concerns and regrets with him.

Stormy also wanted to stop being a drug pusher, but he had high expenses and with no education or skill, he felt trapped. He was introduced to selling cocaine at a young age and had become very successful. Unlike Kevin he was not an addict and was therefore able to accumulate much wealth. Stormy was the only friend that Kevin had, but he was always on the move. However, when he was in town he would find a place for Kevin to sleep.

"The police finally catch Stormy and he is going to jail." One man said to his friend as they sat eating lunch.

Kevin could not believe what he was hearing as he ate the food given to him by the taller man. His only friend and source of cocaine was gone. Stormy had evaded the police for years, but they eventually caught him. Kevin was fortunate to never go to prison, especially when he was distributing drugs for Veronica.

In his time of fame he had houses, but now he lived on the streets or anywhere he could find a little shelter. In his time of fame he had cars, but now he walked around begging. In his time of fame he had plenty to eat and to drink, but now he begged for food and searched through garbage cans hoping to find something to eat.

From fame to failure, Kevin was now just a beggar living on the streets, asking for money from past friends and strangers to get his next high.

13...A Mother's Faith

Stormy's capture by the police was a real shock to Kevin because he depended on him for free cocaine and a safe, warm place to sleep. However, his need for food was greater at the moment, so he got up from his usual sleeping spot, which was by an old dumpster, and walked the streets begging for something to eat or money to purchase a meal.

Kevin had not gone far from the dumpster when a man in long black jacket said:

"Here is some food."

Kevin accepted the food and started eating, but stopped when he realized that the man hadn't walked away. This was the first time ever someone on the streets had given him food and stuck around. Kevin wanted to ask a question, but was too hungry, so he continued consuming the food. After Kevin was finished the man asked him a very important question which would change his life forever.

"What do you want to do with the rest of your life young man?" the stranger asked.

Like the story of the Prodigal Son in the Bible, Kevin replied: "I want to go back home."

"Then follow me," the man suggested and without hesitation Kevin obeyed. The man led him around the corner to a house and knocked on the door. The door was opened by an older man with a pleasant smile.

"Clean this man up and I will be back in two days."

The next two days were the cleanest and most filled days Kevin had in years. Kevin still craved cocaine, but the man was commanded not to let Kevin out of his sight. The man tried to initiate conversation, and they would create small talk, overwhelming Kevin by his kindness. The first man returned after two days as he promised and along with the other man they were able to get Kevin on a plane and to Barbados.

While on the plane Kevin's body shook and

he kept asking for a fix, but the stranger kept insisting: "That won't be possible at the moment."

It was almost three days since Kevin had used cocaine and he was agitated and restless. He had reached rock-bottom, but with the help and kindness of that stranger and nowhere else to go, or no one to turn to, he headed back to Mother's house. The stranger was not going to let Kevin do this alone, so when the plane landed in Barbados he hired a taxi and took Kevin to where mother lived. When they reached the village the man said goodbye and shook Kevin's hand, assuring him that if he was able to fight his own addiction, then Kevin would be able to do so as well.

It had been almost fifteen years since he had returned to the village and to Mother's house. So much had changed, but his head was down and he was too broken to realize the new developments.

Mother was outside in her garden bed when she saw him coming down the gap all shaky and hardly able to walk, and although he was a long way off, she recognized him when no one else in the area did.

"Oh Lord, that looks like Kevie!!" She shouted.

Pops was in the shed when he heard Mother's shout, so he rushed to the front of the house, knocking down a full bucket of milk he had just pulled from Betsy on the way. It was years since he saw his 'son' and the possibility that it was Kevin was too appealing to let anything stand in his way.

"Woman, that is not Kevin. Look how bad that man looks. That can never be Kevin." Pops said and turned to go back to his shed.

"That is Kevin. I know my son." She replied and ran towards him with open arms and welcomed him. She kissed him with tears in her eyes and a trembling in her voice.

"Come now my son. I will take care of you."

Kevin's appearance alone told mother that something was wrong and she squeezed him a little and said

"You will be okay."

This was her boy returning home. She had prayed for this moment for a very long time, just to see her only son again before she closed her eyes and she went the way of the whole earth; but she never thought that it would be under such conditions. Yet not once did she speak a word of condemnation to him; she just hugged and kissed him.

Pops looked at him and simply said: "What happen to you?" Then he returned to the shed, for he could not believe this was the same Kevin in whom he invested all his time and money. He had heard from Jan that they were not together, but she never told him why or that Kevin was a drug addict. It was all making sense why he was not hearing about Kevin and cricket anymore. Pops wanted to really use his cutlass now for sure, and give Kevin two lashes with the flat side.

When Mother hugged him, it felt warm inside his chest and he could not believe it. For many years he had not felt the embrace and compassionate touch of another human being. From that moment Kevin decided that there was no going back to drugs. He had tried before and failed, but with his mother's help he was going to pull through.

The first few months were the hardest. Mother was relentless in her efforts to help Kevin break his addiction.

"No, Kevin you will not have a fix. We have to fight this."

This was an everyday battle between Kevin and his mother. But Mother was big and much stronger than Kevin, and hard as he tried, he could not win with her. She was determined that Kevin would not fail under her watch.

"Just one Ma, please… I can't do without it." Kevin begged, but Mother was determined that Kevin would be freed of this habit. After that thirst for drugs was gone, it was not long before Kevin regained some weight and was starting to smile again. It had been years since he had really smiled, but when he did those around him felt it. These were the smiles of someone who had passed through something and had a voice to speak of it on the other side. Many people that Kevin knew who had fallen victim to drug use and abuse never made it to the other side. Kevin was blessed to make it. He had what the church people called a 'testimony'.

Every day Pops would see him and say nothing. He wanted to say something, but the words seemed to evaporate when he opened his mouth. Kevin sensed it too and would just smile and create small talk, but he knew that Pops was really disappointed in him. As Kevin regained his strength, he would take walks early in the morning to rethink and imagine.

Kevin had disappointed everyone who loved him and along that dark path, created some very bad memories which haunted him daily, therefore forgiving himself was difficult. He had wasted so much time and energy, and had ignored the gift that he was born with. Every now and then depression would step in and zap his strength, leaving him feeling powerless. But these walks allowed him to think about the future and the changes he would have to go through.

This particular morning was one of those days when he had to force himself to walk. He was feeling weary, but he needed to get outside to feel life as it happened all around him so hope will be kept alive in him. As he walked under the branches of Mrs. Thomas' breadfruit tree which overhung the pathway a cocoon fell from a branch and landed in front of him. Kevin bent and picked it up and a tear welled up in his eyes as he gazed upon a picture of his present and future combined. He was at the stage of the worm in this cocoon, but he believe that one day he would emerge as a beautiful butterfly.

14...Forgiven

One early morning Kevin took the back road and ended up by the swamp. The swamp was still there, but it had dried up a bit and many of the trees were cut down except for a few casuarinas trees. As he stood on the hill looking into the swampy water the memory of him being pushed down the hill and into the swamp came rushing into his head, and all he could do was laugh. Following that laughter was a deep sense of pain and regret, because it was there he had met Jan and all the memories of their times together came flooding back. This made him fall to the ground and ask God to forgive him again for hurting the one woman that loved him the most. He was not aware that he was praying aloud when he heard a voice.

"I forgave you a long time ago."

Kevin turned around quickly and saw the most beautiful woman he had ever seen. It was Jan. She was dressed in a long white dress and he thought she looked like an angel.

The swamp was Jan's place of solace since she returned to Barbados. The area had been turned into a recreational park and often she would visit the swamp and sit on one of the benches. She saw when Kevin came and stood on the hill and recognized him, but had hesitated before approaching him. She was not sure if she wanted to talk to him, but the fluttering in her belly propelled her towards him.

"Hello Jan, I did not know you were here." He said, surprised.

"I have been here long enough to hear you pray," she said.

"Jan I was so stupid and I hurt you so much. Please forgive me."

Jan was trying really hard to restrain herself from running into his arms, because there was still a soft spot in her heart for him. But the pain was still there and she needed to say something.

"Kevin how could you do those things to me?"

She asked as tears formed in her eyes.

"I was an idiot," Kevin replied.

Jan continued to pour her heart out to him of all the hurts that she endured and Kevin just held his head down in shame. All he kept saying was:

"I am so sorry."

She could no longer restrain herself, so she hugged him and he wept in her arms as he begged her to forgive him for more than half an hour.

It was a long, hard path of recovery for Jan, but she made it through. She almost died on the journey, but she was a fighter, as her father would always say to her mother when he was alive. "Jan is a tough girl."

All the pain from neglect and being mistreated was dealt a severe blow and Jan was standing tall and strong, determined never to be in that place of defeat again.

Jan had matured so much that Kevin felt like he was talking to a whole new person, and she looked like she had not aged one bit. How could this woman forgive him after all that he did to her? The moment was too intense for Kevin, and he got up to walk away.

"Where are you going Kevin?" Jan asked.

"How could you forgive me Jan? I have hurt you so much."

"There have been times when I was sure the next time I saw you, I would kill you."

"And you just had the perfect chance because I didn't even hear you when you came up behind me." Kevin said humbly.

"It has been a struggle, but God has forgiven me and he asked me to do same for you."

Kevin was overwhelmed that Jan forgave him and as he stared deeply into her eyes and she into his, he wanted to ask: "Are you still the one for me?"

They both knew that words could not express this moment. This was like trying to explain snow to an Eskimo. It needed no explanation. Kevin took her hands in his and asked: "Can we start over?"

Jan hesitated and said: "Not so fast Kevin."

Kevin was a little surprised at her response, but understood and therefore did not pursue the subject. They both needed time to heal and it would take some time for this to happen, so they agreed to spend the following months together praying.

After spending quite a bit of time talking with Jan that day, a weight of guilt was lifted from his shoulders and a new ray of hope was developing. His reality was taking shape and changing in a positive manner, just like all the changes in his old neighborhood, for many of the wooden houses were reconstructed into wall houses, and not many people had pit toilets. By now most had running indoor water and electricity.

Most of the people he knew when he was growing up were still living in the village—people like Ms. Prescott, Mr. Harris and One-foot Mike. It was a nice feeling of being home and seeing familiar people who impacted his early life, yet he was a little sad to see that a lot of the trees were gone and replaced with houses and roads. But that is the price to pay for development, and to him it reflected the change he was feeling on the inside. Every day he was grateful for another opportunity to live.

This was a hard road to travel, but Kevin was determined not to fall again this time. Jan had also made it abundantly clear that this was their last chance to get it right, and if Kevin fell back into drug use, that would be the end of their friendship. She had come too far to settle for a life like before. There would be no more chances after this.

Jan's mother was not too happy about Kevin and her daughter getting back together after what he did to Jan. But Jan was sure that this is what she wanted to do, so eventually her mother respected her decision.

"Jan, thanks for your second touch. My life has new meaning because of it," Kevin told her one day as they sat outside her house on the step.

"You are welcome, but this is a one-time thing. If you ever touch drugs again it is over between us." She said sternly.

Now that Jan was back in Kevin's life, Mother's burden seemed to have lifted. She was smiling more. She could tell that Kevin and Jan were falling in love again. It was something that she wished for herself, but she never had the opportunity, for as fast as Kevin's father was in her life, he was out. She and Pops had raised Kevin, and she was proud to see that not only had her son returned to her, but he was free from drugs and given another chance at life.

"I have prayed for you both." Mother said, "that God would keep you."

All of this was new to Kevin, because Mother had never prayed for him when he was a boy and the feeling was one of happiness. Mother's love for him was now tangible and he welcomed her hugs and kisses and words of encouragement. This was a moment, an experience, a thousand words could not explain. Kevin was on track again with the support of mother and Jan who was back in his life and he promised God that he would never ever use drugs again.

15...Pops

One morning as Pops was milking Betsy he stopped Kevin, who was on his way for a walk. Pops could not restrain himself any longer about the whole thing and was waiting for the right opportunity to talk to Kevin. He felt that this was a good time to let Kevin know how he felt about him messing up his life

"Boy, you is a idiot? Look you almost kill youself and this lovely young lady? What you doing using drugs? And you stop playing cricket?"

Kevin knew his grandfather was right, and although he was a big man, he felt like a little boy being scolded. So he held his head down in shame.

"Sorry Pops." Kevin said.

"Sorry? Sorry kill a man pun a lorry!!" Pops shouted back.

But his grandfather was not finished yet. He had bottled this up for a while and unlike Mother he was not going to let Kevin off the hook so easily. He wished that he could lash him, but he was too old now and was not that strong. But his mouth was still fierce as ever and besides, he was no church person and a few words needed to be said.

"What I told you when you was leaving?" Grandfather asked.

"You said be careful," Kevin replied.

"And you call this careful? Living on the streets and thing? And using that thing that does kill ya brain? I call it playing de ass."

Mother was in the kitchen and had heard enough. "Pops leave the boy alone. He went through enough."

"Enough? He gine stand hey and hear me out." Pops replied.

"No Ma, let him speak." Kevin interjected.

Pops continued to talk about all that he did for Kevin from the time he was a little boy and how he'd had to work hard in the field and raise animals to send Kevin to school when his father left. Pops spoke about how he threatened to cut off Big Bad Billy's head if he ever came near Kevin again. Kevin held his head up when Pops said this. After all these years it was finally revealed what that conversation was about between Billy and his Grandfather.

Kevin just stood there and let his grandfather talk. This was Pops' time of healing. For many years he had felt like he had failed Kevin and that it was his fault that Kevin had chosen a path of drugs.

"Pops, it is not your fault. You raised me the best way you knew," Kevin said, as he felt that was a good time to interrupt.

Pops reached forward and gave Kevin a hug. This was the first time since Kevin's return that his grandfather embraced him, and it was a healing moment for both of them.

Two months later Pops became sick and was unable to speak. It was a most painful and sad time in the Bratts family. Mother was not taking it very well, and would just sit and stare into space. She knew that God was there, but the pain was very great. She knew it would not be long before grandfather died. He had raised her and her brother all by himself when her mother died. She was too young to remember her. Pops was the only parent she knew, and she was losing him.

"Pops knew that his time was near. I felt it too, that is why I let him talk that evening. He couldn't leave this earth with all that guilt inside."

Kevin comforted his mother with these words after Pops closed his eyes one Friday evening with a smile on his face. The pain of letting him go was therefore not as difficult as they would have imagined. They knew for sure that he was on his way to glory, for it was only one day before he became ill that he had confessed Jesus Christ as Lord. At his funeral Kevin spoke on behalf of his grandfather.

> *"Theodore Bratts, or Pops as he was affectionately known by; lived his whole life without God and yet in his last days he received one more chance to surrender his life to Jesus. As a young man he was full of strength and believed that he was invincible and it took him all these years to understand that if we live, we live to the Lord and if we die, we die to the Lord. Theodore Bratts was a fair and honest man. He was not a church*

man, but he demonstrated many of the principles the Bible says we ought to live by. Today we lay to rest my grandfather who was more to me than words can express."

The death of Pops was a great loss in the Bratts family, as he was the one that seemed to hold things together. Mother was getting over the loss slowly, and Kevin spent many days in the shed reflecting on the times he and Pops spent countless hours just being together with the animals.

Now that Pops was gone it was up to Kevin if he would continue keeping the animals or not. Over the years Pops had scaled down the amount of animals he kept considerably. Old Betsy had given birth to young ones and in turn they to other young ones, yet over the years Pops always gave each generation the name 'Betsy'. Kevin missed his grandfather, but during the last times of his life he helped Kevin to be cemented in his decision to never again return to that dark place and stage of his life. His grandfather had taught him to fight and that was what he intended to do. He had an internal drive to become a new man ever day.

16...A Changed Heart

Kevin knew that something was different about Mother. He'd felt it from the first day she hugged him when he walked down the road and how she cared for him, helping him to fight his addiction. He realized that up to this point she had not said one condemning word to him. This was unlike the mother he knew growing up.

In all of his life as a child and even as a teenager he could not remember a time when his mother hugged him or said something kind to him, except the time when he had the house rebuilt and water and electricity installed. But since his return home and recovery from drug addiction she was showering him with kind words. Back then she was always angry and rough. But she had been through something and along the way had found Jesus. She was not even cussing anymore, not even when Ms. Prescott threw garbage over into her yard. All she said was:

"One day that woman will come face to face with Jesus."

One Sunday morning not long afterwards, while Mother was getting ready for church, Kevin heard Ms. Prescott's dog Lion Junior barking strangely. No one would have guessed it was barking at Ms. Prescott, who suffered a heart attack and died right next to the garbage can with garbage in her hand. All Mother said was:

"It's a fearful thing to fall in the arms of a living God."

Mother shared with Kevin that as a little girl she was forced to go to church, but as soon as she became an adult she no longer saw the need for it and had even grown angry at God for giving her a messed up life and a no-good man. For a long time she was bitter and blamed all her problems on others. One day the pastor from the church down the street visited her house and said:

"Good afternoon ma'am. We are having a crusade and wanted to invite you." He was new to the church and the community. In the past there were many crusades, church services, harvest Sundays and other events held at that church, but the former pastors were aware that Mother was not interested in church and had stop inviting her.

"Stop coming hey, cause I ain't coming dey," she had said on a number of occasions, but somehow she found herself entertaining the new pastor as he spoke.

"Will you come?"

"Maybe," she had replied. The very first day of the crusade Mother left her house to go, but changed her mind, and the same thing happened the following night.

"You is a robot or what? Mek up ya mind," Pops had told her.

This happened all the way down to the second-last day, on the last day she entered the church and sat in the back next to Suzie who whispered:

"I hey cause the pastor real sweet and he ain't got nuh wife."

That night mother felt her feet moving without her consent as if they had a mind of their own, dragging her to the front of the church at the request of the pastor who said:

"Who here would like to accept Jesus Christ as Savior?"

That was the changing point in Mother's life and since that night she never missed a Sunday. This was her church. This was where she found the peace that had transformed her life. So she invited Kevin to church. So for the first time in his life he stepped into a church.

The church was not a huge building. It was an old wooden pine building held up on four cornerstones, but there was a peace there that seemed to wrap itself around Kevin. It felt so much like when Mother hugged him, but it was different. It felt stronger. Immediately he felt that warmth again—warmth that he was feeling ever so often now that he was free of drugs.

Pastor Kellman started his sermon. It was the story about the Prodigal Son, but before he could finish and give the altar call, Kevin was up front and on his knees.

"Oh Jesus, I thank you for saving me from drug

use and addiction and giving me another chance at life. Help me to be strong."

As Kevin continued to pray the presence of the Lord was so strong that all he could do was cry, and that he did.

He had never in all his life cried the way he was crying now. Not even when Big Bad Billy pushed him down the hill and into the swamp for lying about him, not even when he lost everything to drugs and was forced to sleep at nights on the streets. He had cried then, but this was a different cry. This was coming from a broken soul. It was so contagious that the whole church started to cry. Even Pastor Kellman came and knelt at the altar and started to cry out to God and ask for forgiveness.

"God I don't know what to do any more. Help and forgive me for doubting your power," he cried out.

Kevin was again becoming somebody important. But this time it was not him, but God working on him to change him to be what he wanted Kevin to be. After church Kevin and Jan approached Pastor Kellman and asked if they could talk with him, and he agreed. They told him of their journey and that they wanted to get married.

"If this is what you want and the Lord approves, who am I to object?" The pastor told them.

17...The Swamp

There was no better place to get married than by the swamp. Everyone was there. Mother was glowing and could not contain her praise. Big Bad Billy came in just for the wedding and Barry was the best man. Bruce stayed home because he still hated Kevin and although Kevin had tried on a number of occasions to make amends, he remained resistant and said:

"I ain't even sorry what happen to you back in New York."

However it was not the time to worry about Bruce. This day was about Kevin and Jan's commitment to each other, so because of this the people of the village who knew of their struggle were happy to come out to the wedding even if they were not invited. But most importantly,

God, who had allowed them to start over, was there. The people who watched on smiled and many who were passing by stopped because this was the first time ever that a wedding was being held by the swamp.

The place was electrified with a sense of joy, excitement and laughter. The grass was cut and the benches beautified with ribbons. The chairs were well placed so that most of the congregation would see Jan as she walked up the hill. Cheers filled the open air as Jan walked up the hill from the swamp signifying the true meaning of their swamp. This was the swamp where they became friends. It was by this swamp that they renewed their friendship and now by this swamp they became one flesh.

Mother surprised Kevin by inviting some of the old cricketers and they came dressed in their cricket gear with bat and ball. It was beautiful. Even the coach from his first big game came to surprise Kevin.

"You a lucky fella, not many people get these sort of chances," he said and gave Kevin an envelope. "Open it later," he said.

Pastor Kellman was dressed in a yellow and

white suit and was looking quite happy with his fiancé by his side. Suzie was not happy with the fact that he had a girlfriend and it was not her. Pastor Kellman began.

"Let's all stand and we will commence this special moment with a prayer of thanks to God for making this occasion possible. Father we want to thank you for these two young persons [the crowd smirked] who have found love and each other again as they join together. May you bless them abundantly."

Then Mother came forward and sang a song. Kevin never knew that Mother could sing so sweetly, and neither did most of the people. God really did transform her from being a cuss-bird to a song-bird.

Pastor Kellman continued.

"Do you Jan take Kevin to be your husband and will love him always?"

She answered "I do."

"And do you Kevin take Jan to be your wife and love her always."

Kevin answered "I do."

"You may kiss each other."Although Kevin had kissed Jan a million times before, this felt like their first and they embraced each other for what seemed like forever. When they finally released each other Pastor Kellman turned to the People and said:

"I now present to you Mr. and Mrs. Kevin Bratts."

As Kevin and Jan stood on a platform that Billy made, they publicly made a commitment to a new life and peace with God. The presence of God filled the air and a sweet scent came upon the light breeze that was now in the tops of the casuarinas trees.

Then Kevin took the microphone from the pastor and thanked everyone for coming.

"I thank you all for being a part of this wedding, it is because of your support that I can stand here and be reunited to the one person who knows me best, my beautiful wife Jan."

After the wedding, as they were on their way home, which was Mother's house, for she had agreed to let them live there until they finished their own home which was not too far away, Kevin seemed a little sad.

"What is the matter hon?" Jan asked.

"I wish that Pops was there to see us," Kevin

answered.

"Pops was there and he was overjoyed for you both," answered Mother.

Exactly six months after the wedding Kevin and Jan entered their home which was constructed with money from Jan, mother, the church and some that Pops had laid aside for Kevin. Just one year short of Jan turning forty, Jan and Kevin were blessed with a beautiful baby boy, and exactly on the same day Kevin turned forty they had their baby girl. Kirk and Janessa were their names, and they were a sign of God's approval and blessing.

18...Uncle Frank

After Pops' death Uncle Frank sank deeper into his drinking, and some days he would not even go to his house which was not far from Mother's. He had moved out years ago or rather was forced out by Pops. When Kevin had heard what happened he had a house built for Frank only because of his cousins who wanted to live with their father, but that was years ago. By the time of Pops' death Kevin's cousins were all grown and had moved out of the village and Frank was totally absorbed in the consumption of alcohol.

The house was falling to the ground because of neglect, and Frank was not even bothered; all that was of concern to him was his next drink of rum.

Kevin was so hurt. He wanted to reach out to

his Uncle. Through the years he had judged him and joined with others labeling Frank as a waste. But after his experience with cocaine addiction, he realized that there was no difference between himself and Frank; it was all addiction, and he wanted to help Frank, but did not know where to start. He knew that his Uncle was in no state of mind for talk. In fact, he could not remember the last time he heard him speak. The men at the shop had given up talking with Frank long ago and would just offer him drinks, which he would take without a response. Ms. Evon, the shopkeeper, allowed him to stay in a corner of the shop until closing time, and would offer him food only because she had great respect for Pops.

"What to do Lord? I want to speak with my Uncle. But I don't know where to start," Kevin prayed.

As soon as he was finished asking the question he heard a voice. He turned around quickly, but there was no one.

"Do for him what that stranger did for you." The voice said.

Kevin dropped to his knees. "How Lord? I have been kind to him before, but it never worked."

"This time you will be doing it in my name," the voice said clearly and distinctly.

Kevin wasted no time. He prayed and asked for strength and headed straight to the rum shop. As he approached his uncle the men gathered to see what would happen because they had not seen Kevin and his uncle speak in years.

"Uncle Frank." Kevin said softly to his uncle who was lying outside on the shop steps.

"What you want?" A voice shouted at Kevin which sounded nothing like his Uncle.

Kevin leapt back and almost fell off the steps. The voice sent chills down his spine and left a strange feeling in his stomach. He knew that this was not going to be an easy battle.

When he was addicted to drugs he needed help, but he did not know where or how to get it. Many times he confided in Stormy but Stormy was in the same boat as Kevin. However, his Uncle didn't want any help, and had said so on many occasions. He was contented with his life, but Kevin knew that this was not how he wanted Uncle Frank to live and die.

Kevin had seen Pastor Kellman speak to demons and command them to come out in

Jesus' name. But he was no Pastor, and did not have that authority or power, as he was told. Then he heard the voice which seemed to be in his head say:

"Use my name."

Reluctantly, Kevin said "In Jesus name."

Uncle Frank started to shake vigorously as he foamed at the mouth. When Kevin saw this, strength and boldness came over him, similar to when he was young and self-confident. But this was different and he shouted:

"IN JESUS NAME COME OUT YOU SPIRIT OF ADDICTION TO ALCOHOL!" and Kevin touched his uncle.

As soon as Kevin touched him he started to cough like a dog's bark and vomited up the most unpleasant smell and liquid Kevin had ever seen. Then he sat up and looked straight into Kevin's eyes and asked in his normal voice:

"Where is Pops?"

"Pops died and went with Jesus." Kevin replied.

"I want Jesus. I feel a big hole in my stomach after I vomited." Uncle Frank said.

After Kevin prayed with him years seemed to

fall off his uncle's face. He looked at least ten years younger. The men who were by the shop all this time were speechless as they observed Uncle Frank's deliverance.

"Pray for me." Old man George begged as he knelt down in front of Kevin.

"Me too," said Peters.

When Kevin was finished at the shop he was exhausted. He certainly was not prepared for that, or so he thought. Neither was Mother, who almost fainted when she heard a voice she had not heard in years. Only one person she knew called her by her full name and that was decades ago.

"Hello Margaret Bratts."

She looked up from her garden bed, and there was her brother standing straight, smiling and talking.

"Thank you Jesus, thank you Jesus," was all that Mother could say. She gave him a big hug and kiss, something she had not done since they were children.

"Jesus found me at last through my nephew," Uncle Frank said.

The following months were filled with

excitement as all the family put their heads together and tried to help Frank build back his life and house.

A father was gone, but his son had returned. There was no time for sadness. There was too much to rejoice over.

19...The Test

Over time Kevin became stronger and confident that he would not use drugs again, and therefore he became an advocate against drug use and its effects on the human body and brain. Soon the word circulated and he was asked to speak about the dangers of drugs at a men's function in another parish. He had just finished speaking and was on his way home when he decided to stop at a local shop to buy bread, and there he saw Veronica. She had returned to Barbados two years ago because she was hiding from someone she owed money to back in New York.

"Hello Kevin," she said.

"Hello," he replied.

"Strange seeing you around here, how are things?" she continued.

"I am good."

Kevin bought his bread, said "goodbye" to Veronica, and left.

Veronica was speechless and felt insulted that Kevin had not carried on a much longer conversation with her, so she ran behind him and caught up with him just before he got into his car.

"Hold up Kevin. I just want to talk to you about before."

"Look Veronica, what happen in New York is behind me now and I am not looking back," he said and got into his car and drove off.

There was a definite change in Kevin and he was determined not to be trapped again by Veronica. She saw that he had indeed changed and she needed to find out all she could about him. Seeing him that day looking so refined reminded her of why she was attracted to him before and she wanted him back. So the next day she sent one of her old buddies, who was also one of Kevin's old friends, to find out all he could and report to her.

"What's up Kevin?"

Kevin turned around, startled to see Timmy the

next day while he was taking his usual morning walk.

"Hi, Timmy. I have not seen you in years. How have you been keeping?"

"I am well, Kevin. What have you been up too?"

"I am free from drugs and serving Jesus," Kevin replied with a big smile on his face.

After talking a bit, Timmy pulled out a bag with some white powder and took a sniff right in front of Kevin.

"You want some? I know you use this, or used to sniff this stuff," said Timmy.

This was the first time since Kevin's 'cleansing' that he came close to drugs. Immediately he felt that urge to take it, but somehow his hand just would not reach out. Without any more delay, Kevin said to Timmy:

"I have to go. As I said, I don't use drugs anymore."

"Once you touch this you can't stop," replied Timmy.

Kevin did not respond. He just got up from the park bench and walked away. This made him painfully aware that he was still a work in progress. He was glad that he didn't take the drugs. This made his resolve even deeper in his mind that he would never again use drugs. That test was just a reminder of his first introduction to crack cocaine. He was weak then, but now he felt a strength and determination that he would not look back, but only forward.

Veronica was not happy with Timmy's report. She wanted Kevin back and she was going to try anything. One night after a meeting, as soon as Kevin got into his car and was about to start the engine, Veronica, who was waiting in the car next to his, opened her door, quickly opened his door, and sat in the passenger seat. Then without one word she opened her dress, revealing her nakedness. In the past he could never refuse her once she was naked, and she was under the assumption that he still could not. It all happened so fast that all Kevin could do was to jump out of his car.

"Are you crazy woman?" Kevin shouted in shock.

She came and stood completely naked in front of Kevin. "I know that you can't refuse this," she said. She didn't care if people saw her naked. She was high, drunk and desperate. Veronica stood with her eyes staring and she smelt of alcohol.

"You need help!" Kevin said.

"Why don't you help me then?" Veronica said in that sensual voice that used to always trap Kevin. She came closer, but Kevin backed away. He was in no way turned on by this crazy display and immediately took out his cell phone to call the police. Veronica realized that her moves were futile and said:

"I will get you Kevin; I did it before and I will do it again."

All Kevin could do as Veronica walked away and got into her car was to fall on his knees and thank God for His strength, because he remembered the times when he was not that strong.

Veronica sped off, almost knocking down a man who was on his way to his truck. She questioned what kind of man Kevin was to have resisted her body. Certainly something had changed in Kevin, but she refused to accept it. She wanted him and she was not going to give up until she had him in her bed again.

Over the following weeks Veronica was

persistent in her efforts to get Kevin back. She would turn up at his meetings and sometimes send notes to his house. Jan couldn't take it anymore, so she went straight to Veronica's house, unknown to Kevin. Veronica was desperate and had purposely moved back to her old village so that she could be near Kevin.

"What is your problem? Leave my man alone."

"Kevin is mine and soon he will come back to me," Veronica retorted.

"If you don't stop I have enough evidence to inform the police," Jan announced.

She turned to walk away when she heard someone shout.

"Look out!"

Jan obeyed immediately to avoid being hit in the head with a bat from Veronica's wild swing.

"So that is how you want it to be?" Jan shouted and with one big swing caught Veronica's jaw and knocked her to the floor. Veronica certainly did not expect that, and Jan had no idea where she got that idea from, but she was on fire and gave Veronica a kick to the stomach.

Veronica surrendered. She had no more fight in her. Jan had made it abundantly clear that Kevin was her man and that she would fight, literally fight who or what threatened to take him away. She lost him once and she would not lose him again. Kevin meant more to her now than ever before, and Veronica saw it in Jan's eyes and said:

"You can have him, he ain't worth it."

"I already do have him and he is worth kicking your ass…" Jan stopped. She had almost lost it for a moment.

Jan returned home and continued her day as if nothing happened. Later when Kevin entered the house she wanted to tell him, but she was waiting for the right time. Night came, yet she said nothing to him about her visit to Veronica's house.

"When are you going to tell me about your wrestling match?" Kevin asked as he confronted her the following morning.

"What match?"

"The one that sent Veronica to the hospital."
"Oh, so you know about that?"

"Yes, and either you are a secret service cop or you work for the defense force or maybe you are one of those ninjas." Kirk said jokingly.

"Oh please… and you are not angry?"

in his chest.

"Go and see the doctor," Kevin had said.

"Later, not now." Billy had responded.

Billy had ignored Kevin's advice because he thought that the pain would go away. The pain did go away, but it was a signal that something was wrong, a signal that Billy overlooked. At the hospital the doctor came into the room and spoke to Billy.

"Sir, you had a mild heart attack. We have done some tests and there is some blockage which prevents your heart from receiving the correct amount of blood. We have to do more tests."

After a few more tests Billy underwent an operation and upon his recovery he was sent home and told to take it easy. But Billy ignored the doctor's advice and because he thought that he was able to play football again, died two months later on the field from a massive heart attack.

Kevin was sad to see his friend go, but as he reflected on Billy, he realized that Billy was an addict to football and although he knew the dangers of playing the sport, he continued anyway. It never occurred to him that people can be addicted to so many things. Pops was addicted to his animals, Frank was addicted to alcohol, and Mother was addicted to cussing. This revelation was fascinating, so that when he was asked to share on the Billy's life at the funeral, he was ready.

> *"Many of you might know that Billy and I were not always friends, and he was a constant enemy when we were boys growing up in this village. However, we settled our conflict and I became his good friend. We have shared some great times together and like many of you it is sad to see him die with such a great future ahead. Billy always told me to tell the truth, so I will do that now. Billy was stubborn and refused to heed to wisdom. So, today his death is a reminder that we all should let wisdom dictate our lives and not our addictions. So rest in peace, my friend and teacher, for you have taught me through your life and death."*

Billy was buried on a cold Thursday morning at the parish church. Many of his football team mates, friends and family were present to bear witness to Kevin's words, as they all knew how passionate Billy felt about football. One thing was certain. He lived a life of forgiveness and he died free of any resentment. He had so many reasons to hate people, particularly his father, but Billy chose to forgive and embrace the calmness in his spirit from a forgiving place.

Billy's father was at the funeral and when he was asked to say something about his son and only child, he refused.

20...New Beginning

Kevin started playing cricket again, but only as the coach for the village team. It felt great to reconnect with his love and passion for cricket. It had been so long since he held a bat or ball and he was humbled yet grateful for the chance to play again.

As he stood on the old pasture with the bat in his hand, immediately as his mind was accustomed to do, he drifted way back to the first time at the age of six when he hit his first ball. Since that time he had always wanted to prove that he was the best, but now, having been through the process, there was no need to prove anything. Kevin had walked a journey and learnt many lessons. Lessons he would never forget.

After a coaching match one Saturday evening

as he and Jan sat on the front porch playing with their children, the phone rang.

"Hello, can I speak with Kevin please?"

"This is Kevin."

This is Ms. Barker, the principal of your old school."

"Yes Ma'am."

"As you know Mr. James the coach has passed away, and I am wondering if you wouldn't mind assisting us in getting the team back on their feet and winning some games?"

"It would be my pleasure," he replied.

This was the same coach that had taught Kevin. It was a feeling of sadness but still of joy to follow in the old coach's footsteps. When the old coach was alive he had gone cold after many years, and the boys were losing the joy of the game. They were constantly losing matches, but with the possibility of Kevin being their new coach and his renewed joy for the game, the boys were excited.

The day of Mr. James' funeral was a sad day for the school and community, but it was also the day when Kevin was recognized as a true leader.

"Today we mark the death and burial of a man

who has served this school and community for over forty years. Rest in peace Mr. James. But today we also mark the near death and new life of our coach Mr. Bratts, who has promised me that he will work hard with the team to bring us out of this string of defeats."

Ms. Barker told the congregation gathered at the parish church.

Kevin was true to his word and with a lot of patience and practice, boys like Chris and Steven who did not want to play cricket were now leading batsmen. Peter, who previously could hardly throw a ball no further than his nose, was now the fast bowler. There were evident and specific gains all around. The girls too were showing a keen interest in the sport and Kevin was by no means going to leave them out. To the amazement of many, Mary and Joy were competing and making more runs than some of the boys.

There were shouts of joy also as the local team won their first match after a series of defeats. With Kevin's assistance as coach, the local cricket team and school team were having great success. It seemed that both the local and school team were in a competition to see who would win the most matches.

21...Not My Glory

These victories caused a stir in the cricket arena as people remembered Kevin and his achievements and wanted to interview him, but he was not interested in the fame anymore. It was all about the players and their achievements. Kevin took the teams forward to accomplish many victories, and although it was not in his heart to be a super star, he felt good for the chance to be good at what he was good at.

Despite his efforts to stay away from the limelight, the media still ran a five-minute clip on the evening news called: *"THE MAN WHO CAME BACK FROM DEATH"*

In that clip they talked about Kevin's early days as a young cricketer and his successes as he grew, but also his addiction to drugs and how

God delivered him from cocaine and now his involvement with the local and school cricket teams. This was a new beginning for Kevin; a chance to show to the world that being a Christian was a joy and a privilege.

Experience is a good teacher and Kevin learnt his lessons well, though the hard way. Kevin taught the students from his life and encouraged them to be the best cricketers they could be; but more importantly the best humans they could be.

"Life is never black or white, there is always a shade of gray that confuses us. This is why it is important to talk to God and have a good friend to confide in."

Kevin said this to the school team as he encouraged them to reach for the stars but never become lost in success.

Many who knew Kevin before he became famous and when he was using drugs could not help but comment on the transformation he underwent and how close he had come to death's door. Kevin himself never hesitated to warn people of the danger of using drugs and of his experience.

The End

Author's Note

Kevin's story is not an unusual one; it is so near to the hearts of so many of us because it echoes what we go through daily. Yours may not be a drug addiction. It may not be an addiction at all. It may just be that life is hard, and that the light at the end of the tunnel has ceased to shine for you. Maybe you might have lost your job or a loved one or just can't cope with the pressure of life. Don't die inside. Find a reason to live, and that light will begin to flicker again and soon burst into a flame because there is always hope.

Many people have given up on life and themselves because they have hit a bump in the road. They have lost control and feel so empty. I know that feeling of emptiness and the urge to quit. But I have learnt over the years that life is never handed without a solution. I believe that

Jesus Christ is that solution, and that he is the hope we need to travel through life's journey. There is no exception. All of us will face some setback at some time or other, but Christ offers the hope that brings the peace in the midst of the storm.

The Bible says that Jesus was in all points tempted as we are, so he is able to help us (Hebrews 4:15). Therefore there is hope.

The enemy of our lives is the devil, and it is his plan to keep mankind in bondage, because he knows that within all of us is the possibility to become great. The further he keeps us away from God, the more we forget that we are created in God's image and we can win.

So many view Christianity as a set of rules, but they never take the time to understand that it is more than that. God is seeking to have a relationship with us. Sin traps us and leads us down all sorts of negative paths that at the time may seem right, but God uses those times to draw us to himself. It is quite often that when we are at our lowest we cry out to him and he responds with love.

God loves us, and although it is such a

familiar phrase, the depth of that love cannot be comprehended by humans. It is his desire to see us prosper and do well. Don't believe the lie that God is out to get us or punish us. On the contrary, God is out to rescue us and save us and turn around every negative event and use it to work in our favour.

As long as there is life, there is Hope.

About the Author

Adrian Harding was born and raised in Barbados. Having been through his early and secondary education, he pursued training which eventually led him to spending some time as a teacher. This allowed him the opportunity to meet many young and older persons who had 'lost their way'.

His desire is to see people both young and old freed from habits and traps that limit their potential. He knows what it is like to struggle and meet obstacles from every direction, therefore he dedicates this book to each of his readers to encourage them to be strong.

www.ingramcontent.com/pod-product-compliance
Lightning Source LLC
Chambersburg PA
CBHW071417300726
48976CB00004B/1150